Puppy Love & Snowflake Kisses

Jennifer Faye

Lazy Dazy Press

Copyright © 2025 by Jennifer F. Stroka

All rights reserved.

No portion of this book may be reproduced in any form without written permission from the publisher or author, except as permitted by U.S. copyright law.

Published by Lazy Dazy Press

Thanks & much appreciation to:

Editor: Lia Fairchild

Cover: Covers and Cupcakes, LLC

About this book...

WHEN SHE NEEDS HELP, he's the last person she would turn to...

Belle Sinclair has recently adopted a stray puppy. It was love at first snuggle. He is the best Christmas present ever. And yet her holiday happiness goes sideways when she hears a siren and spots flashing lights in her rearview mirror.

Sheriff Parker Bishop is a confirmed bachelor. He firmly believes all laws should be obeyed without exception. And so, when he spots the beautiful Belle Sinclair once more committing a moving violation, what choice does he have? He has to pull her over.

But this holiday, Belle's puppy has gone missing. Suspecting foul play, she has to call on the one man in Kringle Falls who can get under her skin with just a look. This Christmas, will they be able to work past their differences in order to help the puppy? And along the way will they find that opposites just might attract?

The Kringle Falls, Vermont, series:
Book 1 – *Puppy Wishes & Candy Kisses*

Book 2 – *Puppy Love & Snowflake Kisses*
Book 3 – *Puppy Smooches & PeppermintKisses*
Book 4 – *Puppy Hugs & Mistletoe Kisses*

Contents

1. Chapter One — 1
2. Chapter Two — 11
3. Chapter Three — 22
4. Chapter Four — 34
5. Chapter Five — 41
6. Chapter Six — 52
7. Chapter Seven — 63
8. Chapter Eight — 75
9. Chapter Nine — 90
10. Chapter Ten — 101
11. Chapter Eleven — 113
12. Chapter Twelve — 128
13. Chapter Thirteen — 138
14. Chapter Fourteen — 147
15. Chapter Fifteen — 162

16.	Chapter Sixteen	171
17.	Chapter Seventeen	179
18.	Chapter Eighteen	192
19.	Chapter Nineteen	200
20.	Chapter Twenty	207
21.	Chapter Twenty-One	219
22.	Chapter Twenty-Two	229
23.	Chapter Twenty-Three	238
24.	Epilogue	245
	Afterword	252
	About Author	253
	Also By	254

Chapter One

"*A*RF! ARF!"

Early on a snowy Thursday morning, Belle Sinclair smiled as she sat crossed-legged on the floor of her living room. Her new puppy, Odie, chased the squeaky ball that rolled across the floor. Playing ball was his favorite activity, aside from giving her kisses.

Odie was a small dog. Only about seven pounds so far. The vet guessed when Odie was fully grown, he'd weigh about fifteen pounds.

No one was quite sure exactly what breeds were in his lineage. Belle suspected there was some poodle in him. He had the softest curly orange fur. He was long and low to the ground, and he had an outgoing personality. He greeted everyone with a wagging tail.

Little more than a week ago, Merry Kringle had introduced Odie into her life. Belle remembered the day she'd received a mysterious call from Merry. When the wife of the town's mayor invited her to stop by, Belle's curiosity had been raised. As soon as she'd stepped into Purr 'n Woof Supplies and saw Odie, she'd fallen in love. There had been no need for Merry to talk Belle into taking him home, because after the first snuggle, it was already a done deal.

Originally, there had been three homeless puppies who had been transported from a shelter in Ohio to Kringle Falls via her new friend, Candi Goodman. At that point, one of the pups, Tank, had been adopted. Belle felt bad about taking Odie and leaving Tater Tot, but Merry told her not to worry. She'd already had the perfect home in mind for him.

Belle never regretted taking Odie home with her. The truth of the matter was that Belle was tired of living alone. After losing both of her parents when she was only eighteen, she'd been on her own. Without any other close family, she made her own family within the close-knit community of Kringle Falls.

Still, there was no one to miss her when she was gone or to be happy when she returned home. And she was tired of waiting around for Mister Right to appear in her life. She was beginning to think that was never going to happen. And so, she was carving out her own life according to her own terms.

Odie ran toward her with the yellow ball in his mouth. He dropped it at her feet. She picked it up and gave it another toss. Only this time the ball went off course and rolled under the Christmas tree. At full speed, Odie charged after the ball. When he tried to stop on the hardwood floors, he ended up sliding. He collided with the tree stand.

The jingle of glass heirloom ornaments filled the room.

Belle jumped to her feet and rushed over to Odie. She got him and the ball out from under the tree. Once she rolled the ball to the other side of the living room, she inspected the ornaments. They all appeared to have survived the collision.

She stepped back and took in the sight of the pink, green, blue, and white ornaments on the tree. They had been handed down through the family. A couple were from her great-grandmother, others were from her grandmother, and a large portion were from her mother. And slowly, she'd been adding some of her own to the collection.

At Christmastime, she loved getting out the decorations because it made her feel a little bit closer to the family that no longer existed. As she stepped back to the couch, she noticed one of the ornaments from the back of the tree had fallen.

She rushed over to the tree and knelt down. Of course, Odie had to see what she was doing. So, while she was on her hands and knees, he was licking her and attempting to jump on her. *What a silly puppy.*

At last, her fingers wrapped around the ornament. When she sat back on her heels, a quick inspection told her it was unharmed. She breathed easier.

The porcelain ornament was in the shape of a little girl holding her teddy bear. Belle ran her fingertips over the ornament with her name scrolled at the bottom. Her mother had painted the small figurine. A sense of longing and loneliness swept over her. She missed her mother a lot.

She blamed herself for her parents not being there to share the holiday with her. She recalled how it was Christmastime eleven years ago. Her parents had been out on the snowy roads when a deer ran in front of the car, and they went over a hillside. Her father had died on impact, but her mother had lived a little longer...

After that, nothing had ever been the same. The life insurance money, of which there wasn't much, went to paying for their funerals and paying off their debts. Not quite out of high school, Belle had to figure out how to make it on her own. It wasn't easy at the age of eighteen to suddenly be in the world all on her own with no safety net available to catch her if she should fall. And she had numerous times, but each time she'd gotten back up and brushed herself off.

The puppy took a mouthful of her flannel pant leg and yanked her back to the present. She blinked away the unshed tears and turned her head to look at him. He stared up at her with those big brown eyes that had gotten him out of so much trouble because he was just sooo cute.

Odie pulled on her pants once more. He still wanted to play. He was a ball of energy, while she was still trying to wake up.

Belle placed the ornament higher on the tree before checking the time. She had a few more minutes before she had to get ready for work. She sat down next to the tree and rolled the ball a few more times.

And then it was time to get on with the day. The puppy ran back to her, dropping the slobbery yellow ball in her lap. When she didn't immediately throw the ball, Odie climbed onto her lap and laid his head down on her thigh. Belle ran her hand down over his downy-soft back.

She lowered her head. "Hey, little boy, I need to get ready for work. I can't be late."

Odie stood up, placing his front paws on her chest. He lifted his head and gave her a sloppy kiss. Her heart swelled with love. They'd only been together a little more than a week, and already she couldn't imagine her life without him in it. They were both orphans who needed each other. He filled a hole in her heart, and she couldn't imagine her life without him.

Belle scooped up the puppy and gave him a hug. "I love you. You'll never be alone again."

Odie leaned into her chest. And for a moment, she just sat there, cuddling him. She felt bad for leaving him home alone, but she would be back at lunch time to let him out and feed him.

The alarm on her smart watch vibrated. It was set to remind her to get ready for work. It was with the biggest regret that she lifted the puppy from her chest.

She turned him so she could look into his big brown eyes. "I'm so sorry, little buddy, but I have to get ready for work."

The puppy let out a whine, as though he understood what she'd just said.

"Okay. You can come with me while I grab a shower and get ready. But then you have to go to your crate." When the pup let out another whine, she said, "I know it isn't fair, but I will be back in no time."

Belle rushed to get ready, which could be difficult with a rambunctious puppy getting into everything. Somehow, she managed to keep him out of things.

When she stepped up to the closet, she couldn't decide on an outfit. Nothing seemed to fit her mood. Running out of time before she was late for work, she tossed the discarded clothes onto the bed. At last, she settled on a blue sweater with a snowman on the front paired with a blue skirt that hit mid-calf.

She moved to her chest of drawers. On top was her jewelry box from when she was a kid. Once upon a time, it had a ballerina inside it that would turn as the music would play. She couldn't remember the last time it had worked. Sadly, after all of these years, the jewelry box was falling apart.

She thought of the antique jewelry box she'd found an estate sale this past autumn. The wooden box had a rose carved in the lid—her favorite flower. It needed a bit of work so she had it stored in the garage until she had time to spiff it up. It shouldn't take more than some sanding and staining it.

Noticing the time, she realized she better hurry. She lifted the lid on the jewelry box and one of the hinges came loose. She sighed. She didn't have time to do anything about it now. She grabbed a snowflake necklace. It would go perfectly with this sweater. And she had snowflake earrings to match.

She scooped up Odie and rushed downstairs. He needed one more trip outside before he went into his crate. She put his red coat on him before they rushed out to the small area she kept shoveled just for him.

However, Odie had no interest in doing his business. Instead, he sniffed every snowflake and then proceeded to stick his head in the snow. Belle couldn't resist a chuckle when the puppy pulled out his snow-covered head. He blinked and then looked at her with those two big brown eyes looking out from what looked like a big snowball on his head. As she laughed, Odie shook himself, sending snow all over her. *Oh, puppy.*

By the time they returned to the house, she was running late. She put Odie into his crate with his comfy cushion and a couple of fleece blankets. He had some toys and a water bowl.

Odie whimpered and sent her a sad puppy face. It was so hard to leave him. "I really do have to go to work if you want more kibble. I love you, little guy. I'll see you in a few hours."

With the greatest regret, she turned away from his pleading eyes. She couldn't be late for work. Not again.

Belle ran out of the little red house that resided on the outskirts of Kringle Falls. As soon as her foot hit the sidewalk, she slipped. Beneath the freshly fallen snow was a layer of ice. Her arms waved at her sides as she regained her balance. She slowed down the rest of the way.

She hopped into her old red Jeep. With a glance in the rearview mirror, she backed out of the gravel driveway and headed to work. Her gaze strayed to the dashboard. She had exactly nine minutes to get there. Every time she glanced at the time, she pressed a little harder on the accelerator.

Mrs. Mavis Thompson was a widow, and she had been Belle's boss since she was in high school. Although Mavis was very kind, she was a stickler for timeliness, and Belle had been late just the day before. It wasn't her fault, but Mavis didn't want to hear any excuses. And now that Belle was trying to convince her to sell her the business when she retired, it was imperative that she impress her.

Belle pulled to a stop at the intersection. After a few cars passed in front of her, she turned right onto Main Street. Frills & Heels Boutique was on the other side of town.

As soon as she made it into Kringle Falls proper, the first traffic light she came to was red. With a sigh, she tramped the brakes. The last thing she needed was to hit all three red lights on her way across town.

Her fingers drummed against the steering wheel. As she waited for the light to change, she glanced around. Fresh snow had fallen the night before, coating the rooftops and awnings. It made Kringle Falls look as though it had been stolen from the front of a Christmas card.

Even though it wasn't even eight o'clock in the morning, the sidewalks were busy. She'd grown up in this town and spent her whole adult life here. But in recent years, city hall had really played up the part of it being a Christmas town—a tourist's destination.

The campaign had really taken off. Their little town was growing. Sometimes, she worried that it was growing too fast. When she was little, everyone in town knew everyone else. These days there were a number of faces she couldn't put a name to. So, their campaign had its pluses and minuses.

Still, Belle couldn't imagine living anywhere else. Her memories were here. Her friends were here. And her future was here. Her main goal now was to buy the boutique when the owner retired. Mavis didn't have any children to leave it to, and she was anxious to be closer to her sister who lived in Florida.

Belle had been saving her money for years. Sometimes more than other times, but her nest egg had steadily grown, and the portion that she'd invested had done really well. Now that she had a respectable amount, she felt as though she could approach a bank for a small business loan without them laughing her out of the place.

The light changed to green. The car in front of her didn't move. Belle tapped her horn. The car inched forward. It appeared they weren't comfortable driving on the winter roads, even though the roads in town had been plowed and treated.

To her relief, the car turned left. She continued straight ahead. She was happy to find the roadway nothing more than wet. Christmas was just two weeks away, and the town was completely decked out in its finest holiday decorations.

As usual, she didn't have any Christmas plans other than to work. Without any family, the traditions from her past had slipped away. Now she watched a lot of holiday movies and occasionally did things with her friends. When she had a boyfriend, she would hang out with him, but after the last breakup didn't go well, she wasn't anxious to enter into a new relationship.

Wee-woo! Wee-woo!

Her gaze flickered to the rear-view mirror and found flashing blue lights. *Seriously?* She let off the accelerator, hoping they would go around her. They didn't. She inwardly groaned. *Not again.*

Chapter Two

*T*HIS CAN'T BE HAPPENING.

With a frustrated groan, Belle put on her right-turn signal and looked for a spot to pull over. When she pulled to a stop, she tried to figure out what she was getting pulled over for. She definitely wasn't speeding, not in this winter weather.

Her gaze strayed to the digital clock on her dash. Only three minutes remained until she was late for work. She stared straight ahead, trying not to get worked up. The calmer she remained, the sooner she'd be on her way. The boutique was only a block away.

After a moment, when the officer still didn't appear at her window, she glanced into the side mirror. He hadn't even gotten out of the car yet. Her gaze returned to the clock. Only two minutes now.

Her hands clenched as the endless waiting continued. This had to be some sort of mix-up. Somehow, she didn't think Mavis would find it interesting.

And then the door of the car behind her opened. *At last.* Belle watched as the officer got out of the car. Even with the wide-brimmed hat hiding part of his face, she'd know Sheriff Bishop anywhere.

His steps were measured. He wasn't in any rush. It was almost like he knew she was now officially late for work. And it was all his fault. He better have a good reason for stopping her.

When he neared her car, she lowered her window. A gust of wintry air rushed inside the car. Yet another reason this stop needed to be brief.

The sheriff stopped next to her door. She couldn't tell what he was thinking because of those tinted sunglasses. She felt as though she were at a disadvantage.

"I wasn't speeding." She'd skipped the pleasantries. They weren't friends, so there was no point in pretending they were.

"For once." His voice was deep and firm.

Not having time for this nonsense, she asked, "Why did you pull me over?"

"Your tail light is out."

"My tail light?" Was he serious? By the no-nonsense look on his handsome face, he was perfectly serious. She struggled to keep her voice neutral. "Thanks for letting me know. Now can I go?"

"Not so fast." He held up his citation book. "Could I have your license and registration?"

"My what?" Surely, she hadn't heard him correctly. "But it's only a burned-out tail light?"

His brows rose. "License and registration."

She was losing her effort to stay calm. He'd just written her a ticket last month. This was starting to get costly.

"You surely aren't going to give me a ticket, are you?" Rushing on, she said, "I mean, I obviously didn't know the light was burned-out, or I would have fixed it."

Without a word, he held out his hand for the requested items.

She frowned at him. It was no wonder they weren't friends. They hadn't been friends in school, and things hadn't changed since they'd graduated. The man was so irritating and such a stickler for following the rules. He never knew what it was to bend rules at times.

Every time she saw him, he was always so serious. Sometimes, she'd swear that if he smiled, his face would crack, which would be a shame because he was quite handsome. Not that she was interested or anything. In fact, if he was the last man alive on the planet, she still wouldn't be interested.

She wasn't sure her car insurance could handle another ticket. They already raised the rates for the past two speeding violations. The first ticket had been last summer when she was three miles per hour over the limit. The second time was just last month when she was four miles per hour over. It was why she kept a close eye on her speed when she was in town. In fact, she now drove below the speed limit. And that was why getting pulled over this time really bothered her.

Still, her mother used to say: "You can catch more flies with honey than with vinegar." So, Belle tried to put some honey in her voice. "Couldn't you just let it pass this time?" She forced a smile to her lips. "After all, I was under the speed limit."

He arched a brow at her. "You should always drive the speed limit. You shouldn't get rewarded for following the law."

No wonder this guy was still single. With a huff, she reached for her purse and grabbed her wallet. She held it out to him.

"Please remove your license."

She didn't want to do anything to help him write her a ticket. But she didn't have time to drag this out. She was certain her boss was wondering what had happened to her. She yanked out her license. Without even looking at him, she held it out.

"And your registration."

With another sigh, she leaned over and opened the glove box. A bunch of white napkins filled it. It'd been a while since she'd cleaned it out. She'd been distracted since she'd gotten the puppy.

She yanked the napkins out and placed them on the passenger seat. After tossing a few more things on the seat, she finally located the registration card. She handed it over to him.

"I really need to get to work," she said.

"I'll just be a moment." He walked away.

Seriously? She couldn't believe he was dragging this out. Couldn't he just write the ticket and be on his way? *No.* He had to take his good old time. It wasn't like she had anywhere to be or anything.

She put up her window. With a huff, she watched in the rearview mirror as he got into his cruiser with the lights still flashing, as if enough people hadn't noticed that she had been pulled over *again*. This was humiliating.

Her fingers drummed on the steering wheel. What was he doing? Running her plates? Checking her ID for any outstanding warrants?

She'd have gladly told him that he wouldn't find anything. The only place she had any tickets was in Kringle Falls. And the only officer who insisted on pulling her over was him. It was like he had it out for her or something.

At last, he walked back to her car. He was just about to hand her license and registration back to her when her phone rang. A quick glance at the screen on her dash let her know it was her boss. *Oh, boy. This is not good.*

"You can have these." He handed over her cards.

As she put them away, she caught him writing something. Probably how much she now owed city hall or whoever collected the fines.

He tore off the ticket but before he handed it to her, he said, "You really need to get that light fixed as soon as possible. With the bad weather that's supposed to blow in, you don't want a tail light out. It isn't safe." Then he handed her the ticket. "Have a good day."

A good day? Is he serious? He wrote her a ticket, and she was late for work. What was good about any of that?

Without taking the time to read the ticket, she tossed it onto the passenger seat with the heap of napkins. She put the car in drive and resisted the urge to tramp the accelerator. Instead, she put on her turn signal and then calmly merged into traffic.

When she reached the boutique, she drove around to the back, where there was a small parking lot. She turned off the engine, and since she was already late, she took a moment to gather her thoughts. She was still steamed over the fact that Sheriff Bishop had pulled her over and proceeded to write her a ticket for her tail light being out. Couldn't he have just let her know and let it go at that?

Now that she was late, Mavis would give her a hard time about leaving for lunch. And she had to step out because she had the puppy at home counting on her to give him a potty break. With a sigh, she grabbed her purse and phone. She got out of the car and closed the door.

She turned and took a step. Her foot landed on ice. In the next instant, her feet slipped out from under her. It happened so fast the next thing she knew, her backside smacked the ice. *Ouch.*

She groaned. This day was totally against her. What was it her mother used to say? That bad things came in threes. She was late for work. She got pulled over. So, did this make her third bit of bad luck? She hoped so.

A car door closed in the alleyway. Before she could get to her feet, she heard a familiar voice.

"Belle, are you all right?" Sheriff Bishop rushed to her side. "Do you need an ambulance?"

He was the very last person she wanted to see, especially in this awkward situation. She frowned at him. "I'm fine."

When she tried to stand up, her feet slid across the ice. It appeared the whole parking lot was nothing but a sheet of ice. The cold and dampness seeped through her skirt. Not only was she late, but she was going to look like a mess too. It appeared her bad luck just kept rolling along.

The next thing she knew there were capable hands wrapping around her and helping her to her feet. She was grateful to be off the ice, but she wasn't happy for his help. They weren't friends. They weren't even friendly.

"What are you doing here?" She pressed her hands to her hips, ignoring the tender bruise forming on her left side. "Are you following me?"

He frowned at her. "I didn't really expect a thank you, but I don't deserve that accusation."

Her gaze searched his. She refused to acknowledge the way his intense stare made her heart beat faster. Instead, she focused on her suspicion that he'd followed her. But why? She'd noticed he hadn't directly answered her question.

Her gaze narrowed on him. "Why are you following me?"

A lopsided smile formed on his lips before he shook his head. She hated the way her breath caught in her throat as she stared at him. He was undeniably handsome. But it wasn't enough to overcome the way he'd irritated her since they were kids. And she wasn't going to think about the time he'd gotten her disqualified from a school track meet because her foot had accidentally been over the start line.

"I wasn't following you." His tone was matter of fact. "As you know, I patrol the town, and it's a small town. We are bound to run into each other."

It was true this was a small town. At times like this, it was too small. She had no choice but to accept his words.

"Fine. I have to go to work." She paused. "Unless you plan to give me another ticket."

His brows lifted high on his forehead. "No. No ticket this time. But make sure you get that light fixed."

"I will." And then she straightened her shoulders and carefully walked away.

She slipped a couple of times, but she remained upright. And though she didn't look over her shoulder, she sensed him staring at her as she walked away. She was tempted to glance back at him, but she refused to let him know that his presence got to her.

She opened the back door and let herself inside. Over the speaker system, she could hear "It's the Most Wonderful Time of the Year." This morning, she didn't know if she agreed with the song.

As she slipped off her coat and hung it up, she heard the click of heels on the tile floor. Belle braced herself to deal with her boss. She hurriedly shrugged off her winter coat and hung it up.

No sooner had she done that when her boss approached her. Her gray hair was pulled up in her standard bun. And her ivory face was made up, but there was a frown on it. "You're late."

"I'm so sorry. Everything that could go wrong this morning did go wrong."

Mavis arched her penciled brow. "You know I don't care for excuses."

"Yes, ma'am. It won't happen again."

"It better not." Mavis gave her clothes a once-over. "What happened to you? Your skirt is wrinkled and...and wet."

Belle sighed, and her shoulders drooped. "I fell on the ice in the parking lot."

"Oh, no." Her boss's brows rose, and then with genuine concern in her voice, she asked, "Are you all right?"

Belle nodded, although she was quite certain her hip was going to have a big bruise by morning.

"That was supposed to have been taken care of." Her brows drew together as her frown deepened. "I'll call Frosty Plows. They better get someone here right away." A look of concern came over her again. "Are you sure you're all right?"

"I'm fine. I promise."

Thankfully, Mavis lived above the boutique and had no reason to be in the parking lot. At her age, a slip and fall could be very serious. For the last several years, the winters had been getting to her. She said that her joints didn't work so well when the temperature dipped. She'd been talking about moving to Florida to join her sister.

Wanting to reassure Mavis that everything would be all right, she said, "They're probably running behind after the big snow last night."

"Probably. But I can't have people getting injured out there. Look at you. You could have broken something."

Belle glanced down at her clothes. The side of her blue skirt was covered in muck. And there were a couple of tears. She inwardly groaned. It was beyond repair.

She glanced over at her winter coat. It had taken the brunt of her fall, but it didn't appear to be damaged—just a bit dirty, but that was easily remedied. It had protected her navy-blue sweater with a big snowman with a red cap and orange nose. She'd bought it last year from the clearance rack, and this was the first time she'd worn it.

"Stay right there," Mavis said. "I'll be right back."

Belle looked down at her skirt again. This was her favorite skirt. It matched her sweater perfectly. She rushed to the bathroom and grabbed a couple of paper towels. She dampened them before rushing back to the spot where she'd agreed to wait for Mavis.

Her boss returned. "Here." She held out a blue skirt. "Put this on."

"Oh. Uh…" She noticed that it wasn't one of the cheaper skirts from the clearance rack. In fact, this skirt was part of the new inventory. It was dark blue denim that ended mid-calf. It had embroidered snowflakes along one side. Belle recalled admiring it when she'd hung it on the rack. It would go perfectly with her sweater.

"Go ahead." Mavis gave the skirt a quick shake. "Take it. It's the least I can do after you got hurt."

"I, uh..." Belle was caught off guard by her boss's generosity. "Thank you."

"Can I get you anything else?"

Belle shook her head. "I'm good. Thank you."

Just then the jingle of the front door could be heard. Mavis looked at her. "I'll take care of that. You get changed."

Belle retreated to the bathroom to get changed. She was touched that Mavis had given her the skirt. Maybe it was time to broach the subject of buying the shop.

Although, today probably wasn't the right time. She was still shaken from being pulled over by the sheriff and being ticketed right there in the middle of town. With the way gossip made the rounds, the news would be all over town before lunch.

As Sheriff Bishop came to mind, she frowned. Why did he have to zero in on her? Weren't there other people in town that deserved tickets?

Whatever. She would just keep her distance from him. She knew that was easier said than done, considering Kringle Falls was such a small town. But it wouldn't stop her from trying to avoid him.

Chapter Three

That hadn't gone well.

Not at all.

Parker didn't intend for things to get confrontational with Belle. He'd merely been trying to help her out with her tail light. She'd certainly taken it the wrong way.

She didn't even seem thankful that all he did was give her a warning to get it fixed. He could have just as easily fined her. It wasn't like this was the first time he'd pulled her over.

Belle had a lead foot in her red Jeep. Although her speeding hadn't been in downtown, it was still illegal to speed on the outskirts of town.

He sighed. At last, his shift was over. Now he could go home and spend some time in his woodshop. He was finishing a wooden bench for his mother to put in her foyer. It was going to be a Christmas present.

First, he needed a cup of coffee. He stepped into Kringle Cup Café. He ordered a large coffee with milk. It would get him through a couple hours of staining.

On his way out of the coffeeshop, he heard someone call out his name. He turned and looked around. That was when he spotted his younger brother Michael. His brother waved him over to the table, where he was sitting alone.

Not in any particular rush to get home, Parker walked over and took a seat. "Hey, what are you doing here?"

"Waiting for Candi to get done at Purr 'n Woof. We're supposed to go do a little Christmas shopping."

Parker arched a brow. "You two are getting serious?"

Without hesitation, Michael nodded. "I guess when you know it's right, it is."

"I'm happy for you."

"Maybe you should think about getting serious with someone." Michael's gaze prodded him.

Parker shook his head. "I don't think so. Besides, who would I get involved with in this small town?"

"How about the one woman who has been getting under your skin since we were kids?"

"I don't know who you're talking about." The words came rushing out much faster than he'd intended. The truth of the matter was that he knew exactly who his brother was talking about—Belle Sinclair. The beautiful woman who always knew how to push his buttons.

But his brother had it all wrong. They rubbed each other the wrong way, even when he was trying to help her out. There was no way they could go out on a date much less have a serious relationship. The thought was laughable. So, then, why wasn't he laughing?

He gave himself a mental shake, removing the thought of him getting involved with Belle. That wasn't going to happen. Not a chance.

An amused look came over Michael's face. "When you start denying things so vehemently, I know you're lying. The question I have is: are you lying to me or to yourself?"

"I'm not lying." His voice wasn't as firm as he would have liked it to be.

A grin came over Michael's face. "Uh-huh. And is that why you pulled Belle over again and wrote her another ticket?"

Parker's frown deepened. "How do you know?"

"Because you pulled her over in the middle of town. You know this place loves gossip. And each time you pull Belle over, the tongues wag. They can't decide if you hate her or if you're in love."

"What? I'm not in love with her." His voice rose in volume. When he glanced around, everyone was staring at them. Heat rushed up his neck and settled in his face. He made a point to keep his voice low. "Stop with this Belle stuff."

Michael looked at him with amusement dancing in his eyes. "Then, why don't you get yourself a date? It might stop the gossip. Then again, it might start new gossip."

Parker shook his head and waved off his brother from continuing. "Just stop. I'm done with dating. I'm fine being a bachelor."

Michael arched a brow, as though contemplating his words. "All right. But how about you try to be Belle's friend. If you give her a chance, you'd find out that she's really nice."

He wanted his brother to stop talking about Belle. "And why would I want to do that?"

Michael let out a laugh. "The fact you have to ask me says it all. Just find a way to strike a truce with the woman. I'm sure she would appreciate it more than you pulling her over every chance you get."

"Hey, I only pull her over when her actions warrant it."

Michael grinned at him. "Uh-huh. You keep telling yourself that. Rumor has it that you pulled her over last time because she was going two miles over the speed limit."

"It was four over, and she was breaking the law." He didn't like the feeling of being on the defensive with his brother. "Why are you attacking me?"

"I'm not. But if you're feeling attacked, maybe it gives you some idea how Belle must feel."

Is that the way Belle felt? He honestly never stopped to consider it from her perspective. His brother had certainly given him a lot to think about.

Parker should let it go but he couldn't, not yet. "Do you really think she feels that way?" When Michael shrugged, Parker said, "I don't want anyone to hate me for doing my job."

"Then perhaps you should make a friendly gesture."

A friendly gesture? His mind raced. "Like what?"

"I don't know. That's for you to figure out." He looked past him. "There's Candi. I have to go. But you might question why you don't date much and why you seem to find yourself paying special attention to Belle's driving habits." Michael grabbed the two to-go cups in front of him and headed for the exit, where Candi was waiting for him.

When she caught Parker's gaze, she smiled and waved. Parker waved back. Just because things had worked out so well for his brother, didn't mean it would work out for him too—and certainly not with the girl who used to always snub him in school.

Still, all of that stuff was far in the past. Maybe it was time to try to make peace with Belle. Not that he was giving his brother's comments any credence. It was just that Belle seemed like she could use a helping hand with the burned-out light.

With the thought in mind, he stood. He grabbed his coffee and headed for the door. He had a destination in mind. He just wasn't sure if what he was about to do was a good idea. If it all blew up in his face, he'd blame it on his brother.

It had been a busy day.

And it wasn't over yet.

Belle had rushed home at lunchtime. Odie had barked like crazy when she walked in the door. His butt wiggled as his tail swished back and forth like a windshield wiper on full speed.

She didn't stay long. She couldn't run late, because she couldn't speed on the way back. She wasn't giving Parker one more chance to write her a ticket. Although, she still had the light out. Surely, he didn't expect her to take off work to fix it. Even he couldn't be that exacting, could he?

She made it back to Frills & Heels without any run-ins with the sheriff. The afternoon moved along swiftly. Belle checked out their latest customer and sent her off with a Merry Christmas. People were stopping in to buy clothes for the holidays. The store's clothes were tailored to the over-thirty and young-at-heart crowd. They did a steady business with peaks at the holidays and the summer. Someday, Belle would like to carve out an area for the twenty-somethings too.

She checked the big clock on the wall behind the checkout counter. Thirty-three minutes to go. And then she had a tail light to deal with. Honestly, she didn't have a clue how to change it. Normally, she'd take it to We Fix It Auto, but they were closed until after the New Year. It was a good thing they had videos online to show her what she needed to do.

And then she had another thought—she didn't have a replacement light bulb. She'd swing by Merry Mufflers & More on the way home and pick up the light bulb. She just hoped they could tell her which size she needed.

With this being a small town, the businesses closed early and people went home for dinner. She better check what time they were open until. She pulled it up on her phone and found that they'd already closed at four o'clock. She sighed. There was no way she could fix it tonight. Knowing her luck, Sheriff Bishop would notice and give her yet another ticket.

The jingle of the front door drew her attention. She looked up to find two women walking in. They appeared to be together. With Mavis already busy helping another woman, Belle stepped forward.

"Welcome to Frills & Heels. My name's Belle. How may I help you?"

The older of the two women, who had a brunette bob, stepped forward. She smiled. "We're looking for something to wear to a Christmas party."

As she showed them clothing items that might be just what they were looking for, she momentarily forgot about her problems and instead focused on the task at hand. This was the part of the job she loved, interacting with the customers. With the town being a tourist destination, she was constantly meeting new people, many of whom had entertaining tales to tell.

She had just walked the ladies back to the changing rooms when she heard her boss calling her name. Belle had no idea what she wanted, but she was curious. Usually Mavis didn't bother her when she was working with customers.

When she stepped back into the front of the boutique, her gaze collided with Sheriff Bishop's. The breath stilled in her lungs. What was he doing here?

If he was here to give her a hard time in front of her boss, he could think again. She strode toward him. Lowering her voice, she asked, "What are you doing here?"

His brows rose, as though he was surprised by her hostility. "I need your car keys."

"What?" Surely, she hadn't heard him correctly.

"I need your keys."

Her gaze narrowed as she crossed her arms. "What are you planning to do? Have my car towed?"

A lopsided smile eased the lines on his face. In that moment, she was reminded of how cute he was. All of the Bishop brothers were good-looking, but Parker was by far the handsomest. Too bad he was so annoying.

This wasn't going like he'd imagined.

Parker had thought she would be relieved to have the light fixed. Instead, she was eyeing him with suspicion. Maybe he had been a little hard on her lately. Maybe it was because she drew his attention every time she was out and about.

They'd been doing this hostile thing for so many years they didn't know how to act any different around each other. Perhaps it was time to change that. But was it too late?

"Relax." His voice was soft. "I just came to do you a favor."

She looked at him with suspicion. "I don't need you to do me a favor."

He sighed. Maybe his brother had a point. "Listen, I'm sorry if it seems like I'm pulling you over a lot." When her eyes widened in surprise, he said, "Just slow down."

She leveled her shoulders and stared directly at him. "I did slow down, and you still pulled me over for a light being out. For your information, I didn't even realize it was out."

"And did you look at your ticket?"

She was quiet for a moment. "No."

He nodded. That was what he figured. "If you would let me have your keys, I can go fix your tail light."

Her gaze narrowed. "Why do you want to help me?"

He shrugged as he tried to find an answer. "Let's just say that I'm in the holiday mood. Besides, Merry Mufflers and More is closed now. You'd have to drive home with your light out."

"And you'd have to ticket me again." She rolled her eyes.

"Belle," her boss called out to her. "Your customer needs your assistance."

With a sigh, Belle rushed back to the checkout counter. She reached beneath the counter and then returned to hold out a set of keys to him. "How much is this going to cost me?"

"Nothing."

She dropped the keys into his hand and rushed to the back of the boutique. So much for a thank you. Then again, that wasn't the point of this exercise. It was to get his brother off his back.

———ele———

This was the longest twenty-four minutes ever.

At last, the work day was over. After Belle's two customers left, the boutique grew quiet. They were able to get through their closing process and out the door at precisely five o'clock. For Mavis that meant going upstairs.

For Belle, it meant heading out in the cold, snowy evening and facing Parker. She couldn't believe he'd volunteered to change the light in her car. He was up to something, but what?

She grabbed her purse from under the counter. She moved swiftly to the back of the store and slipped on her boots before shrugging on her winter coat. At the back door, she drew in a deep breath and let it out. She opened the back door and headed toward her car.

There were large snowflakes drifting ever so gently to the ground. Her gaze moved to her car, where she found Sheriff Bishop leaning against it while staring at his phone. When he lifted his head and his gaze met hers, her stomach dipped. She refused to decipher her reaction to him staring at her.

And then a slow, lazy smile pulled at his lips. The breath caught in her lungs. She averted her gaze. She didn't care how handsome he was; she wasn't going to let her guard down with him. He'd probably find another reason to pull her over tomorrow or the next day.

She came to a stop a respectable distance from him. "You're still here?"

He nodded. "I thought you'd want these back." He dangled the keys in front of her. After she took them, he said, "Hop in. I want to make sure the light works."

Not sure what to say, she quietly did as he asked. She started the engine. The lights automatically turned on. She put down the window.

"Looks good," he said. "Press the brakes."

A moment later, he stood next to the window. "It all looks good now. You shouldn't have any more problems."

"Don't you mean any more tickets?" It still irked her that he was always finding a reason to write her up.

He smiled again. "You shouldn't have to worry about those either...as long as you lighten up on the gas pedal."

"I don't get it." She studied him. "Why are you being nice to me?"

"Believe it or not, I'm not such a bad guy."

She opened her mouth to disagree but ended up closing it without saying a word. She told herself it didn't matter. They were never going to be friends. They'd had their chance many years ago. If it was meant to be, it would have worked out then.

"Well, uh... Thanks." She didn't know what else to say.

"You're welcome. And have a good evening."

She pulled out of the parking lot and found herself glancing in the rearview mirror. She saw Parker's figure moving in the opposite direction. What was up with him? Why had he helped her out? She pondered those questions the rest of the way home.

Chapter Four

Christmas was eight days away.

The following day, business at the boutique had tapered off late in the afternoon, allowing them to close a little early. Thankfully, it was Friday, and Belle was on her way home. All she wanted to do was curl up on the couch with Odie and watch a feel-good holiday movie while the snow fell outside.

She parked in the driveway. When she reached for her purse on the passenger seat, she noticed the mess of napkins from the other day when Parker had pulled her over. She would clean them up later.

She got out and headed for the front door. When she stepped up onto the porch, she came to a halt. The front door was open a few inches.

Her heart lurched into her throat. Her mind raced as she tried to come up with a reason her front door would be hanging open. She was one hundred percent certain she'd closed and locked the deadbolt when she'd left after lunch.

Was there someone inside? She didn't know what to do. If she called the cops and there was some reasonable answer for why her door was open, she'd look ridiculous. But if there was a criminal in her house, she didn't want to face them alone.

As she contemplated her next steps, she tiptoed to the opening in the door. She peered inside but didn't see anyone. She paused and tried to hear over the pounding of her heart. There wasn't a sound coming from inside. There wasn't even so much as a whimper from Odie. If someone was in the house, Odie would normally be barking his fuzzy little head off.

With that thought in mind, she pushed the door open wider. "Hello. Anyone here?"

She paused and listened again. Still no sounds.

Her heart was hammering, and her chest was tight as she took a step into the house. Normally, she took her snow boots off at the door but not today. If she had to flee, she wasn't running out into the snow in her socks.

"Hello?" She held still, waiting and listening.

There was no sound. No footsteps. Nothing at all. Just the pounding of her heart echoing in her ears.

And then dread blossomed in her chest. It was a suffocating feeling that grew with each breath. Her house hadn't been this silent since she'd brought Odie home.

Every day when she crossed the threshold, Odie would emit an excited bark. This evening, there was no bark, no yip, no nothing. Belle ran to his crate in the corner of the living room.

Before she even reached it, she knew it wasn't good. The door was hanging open. She knelt down. The crate was empty except for Odie's favorite toy—a stuffed lamb that he loved to squeak. Odie and Lambie were practically inseparable.

She straightened. "Odie! Here, boy!" She prayed that he'd come running to her with his little tail swishing back and forth. "Odie! Time to eat." It wasn't really, but she'd gladly feed him early if it meant finding him safe and sound. "Odie, please. Come here."

The only sound was the winter wind whipping through the open doorway. Tears burned at the back of her eyes. What was going on?

There was absolutely no way that she'd left both the crate door and the front door open. No chance at all. Someone had been here. Her blood ran cold.

But who? And did they take Odie? Or had he wondered off on his own? It was unlikely. Odie didn't like the cold. He'd much rather spend his time stretched out in front of the fireplace.

She continued looking around. It wasn't until she reached the kitchen that she found her cabinet doors and refrigerator hanging open. But why?

When she went to close the fridge because it was a natural instinct, she came across a note on the kitchen island. The breath hitched in her lungs. It read:

I'll be in contact.

It was written sloppily on a napkin with a black maker. There was no name. No hints about who had invaded her home and dognapped Odie.

She had to get her furbaby back. She reached for her phone, which was in her coat pocket. She dialed nine-one-one.

"This is nine-one-one. What is your emergency?"

"My house... It's been broken into. And they, uh..." Her heart ached to say the words out loud. "They kidnapped my dog."

"Is anyone hurt?"

"No. I wasn't home at the time."

"What's your address?" After Belle told her, the operator said, "I have units dispatched to your location. Don't touch anything until they reach you. Do you feel safe?"

"I..." Did she? Not really. Someone had invaded her personal space. She felt naked and exposed. "I don't know."

"Do you have somewhere safe you can wait?"

Her mind raced. "My car?"

She retraced her steps and put the front door back the way she'd found it. Once in her car, she started the engine and cranked up the heat. Even with the heat blowing directly on her, it didn't warm her.

She sat there, trying to think of who would take her dog and why. Poor Odie must be so scared and wondering where she was. The tears rushed back to her eyes, and this time no amount of blinking was going to stop them. They splashed onto her cheeks.

This had to be a horrible nightmare, and soon she'd wake up. But no matter how much she wished that were true, it wasn't. She was stuck in her very own live and in color nightmare.

Flashing lights filled her rearview mirror. A car pulled up behind her. She wondered if it was Sheriff Bishop. She couldn't decide if his presence would make her feel better or worse.

Belle swiped at her cheeks before getting out of the car, hoping they would be able to help her find Odie. The poor little guy.

Deputies Luke Williams and Paula Stark approached her. Deputy Stark was the first to speak. "Hey, Belle. Are you okay?"

Belle nodded. Physically, she was fine, but she'd been shaken to the core by this break-in. The fact that someone would barge into her house was bad enough, but for them to take her dog was unbearable. Who does such a thing?

"What happened?" Deputy Stark asked.

"Someone broke into the house. They took my dog."

"Did they take anything else?"

"I..." Her mind drew a total blank. "I don't know. As soon as I knew Odie was gone, I called you guys."

The deputy nodded. "Are you sure whoever was in there is gone now?"

"No. I just assumed they were gone because Odie wasn't there." She supposed it was possible there was more than one burglar. The thought sent a chill down her spine.

"You stay here," Deputy Williams said. "We'll clear the house."

Belle once more nodded her head. They didn't have to tell her twice. Before she could climb back into her car and out of the frigid air, another car pulled up to her house.

Her first thought was that it might be the dognapper returning to the scene of the crime. In the next breath, she realized there was a police car sitting in her driveway. And even though the flashing lights were off, it was still obvious. No one would be dumb enough to come snooping around with the cops there.

She squinted into the dark, trying to make out who was in the car, but with a moonless sky, it was too dark to make anything out. She wasn't sure what to do, so she stood there. Eventually, the person got out of the car. They were tall and had broad shoulders. Definitely a man.

The breath hitched in her lungs as she waited to learn if he was friend or foe. It wasn't until they were about ten feet away that she was able to make out that it was Parker. The pent-up air whooshed from her lungs. She was never so happy to see him—and that was saying a lot.

"Belle, are you all right?" His tone held a genuine note of concern.

She was caught off guard at his concern. She was beginning to think they would be at odds for the rest of their lives.

She nodded. "I am, but Odie isn't."

Just then she heard footsteps behind her. Belle turned to the approaching deputies. What did they learn? A clue to where Odie had been taken?

"The house is clear," Deputy Williams said. "Whoever broke in is long gone."

"Hey, boss," Deputy Stark said. "I thought you had the evening off."

"I thought so, too, but plans change." Parker planted his hands on his trim waist.

Belle noticed how he didn't bother to explain his appearance at her house. She couldn't help but wonder if he normally showed up at scenes on his evening off. Or was she a special case?

Chapter Five

This was a first.

A dognapping in Kringle Falls.

Parker quite honestly never had a case like this one. There were protocols for human kidnappings. They would call in the state police and the FBI, but that wasn't going to work for a dognapping.

He and the deputies walked the scene while he had Belle wait in her car. He didn't want her with them, because there was just something about her that inevitably distracted him.

Normally, he'd let his deputies handle the call. If they needed him, they knew to call. But when he'd heard the call go out over the scanner, he recognized the address from Belle's driver's license. He knew she was in trouble, and he'd grabbed his keys and headed out the door.

When he was satisfied that Belle's house was secure for the moment, he had her join them in the living room. He had her repeat the events that had led her to call nine-one-one.

"So, you think whoever broke in took your dog?" he asked.

"I know they did." She led them to the kitchen, and there on the island was a handwritten note.

When she went to pick it up, he stopped her. "We'll need to check it for fingerprints. Did you pick it up before?"

She opened her mouth to answer but then wordlessly closed her mouth.

"It's okay if you did," he said. "We'll just need to take your fingerprints for elimination."

Worry lines creased her beautiful face. "I... I don't know. I can't remember."

"It's okay. We'll get this figured out." He turned to Deputy Stark. "Can you bag and tag this? Then I want you both to go outside and check the perimeter. See if you see any footsteps or any other signs that someone has been here."

Once they left, he turned back to Belle. He could tell by the torment in her eyes that she loved her dog very much. "Are you absolutely sure that you closed and locked the front door? Is there any chance you were in such a rush to get back to work that you forgot to close it?"

She frowned at him. "Really? You're trying to blame this on me. You think that I played a part in my Odie being dognapped?"

He shook his head. That wasn't what he was implying. But from the deputies' accounts of the inside, there were no other points of entry. This was done either by a professional, which he didn't think was the case, or by someone she knew—someone who knew her routines and their way around the place. He tried again. "Think about it. Is there anyone that has a key to your house?" When she shook her head, he said, "Do you leave a key outside, like under a mat or in one of those little garden decorations?"

She once more shook her head. "No. I haven't done any of those things."

He frowned. "Do you have a boyfriend?"

"No."

He ignored the happiness that zinged through him upon learning that she was single. After all, he had a job to do. Besides, Belle was all wrong for him. She didn't follow the rules, she was stubborn, and the one time he'd asked her out, she'd shot him down.

Pushing those thoughts to the back of his mind, he said, "Can you look around and tell us what's missing?"

"You mean besides Odie? Because he's all that I really care about." When the sheriff nodded, she said, "I... I'll try."

He followed her gaze to the dog crate. As she stared at its emptiness, there was a vulnerability that showed in her eyes. It was all he could do not to go to her and hold her in his arms. He wanted to assure her that everything was going to be okay.

But the professional part of him knew he couldn't do that. First, he didn't know if it would all work out for the best. And second, he had to maintain a professional distance.

Instead, he directed her attention away from the dog crate. "Is there anything missing from the mantel?"

Her gaze hesitated before moving toward the mantel. After a moment of sweeping her gaze across the collection of snowmen in all different sizes, she shook her head. It was then he directed her to the next area to search.

He noticed how her house was completely decked out for Christmas. He couldn't help but wonder if she was one of the residents who kept the decorations up year-round, since Kringle Falls had been deemed a "Christmas Town." Their claim to fame grew each year, drawing in more tourists. On one hand, it was good for Kringle Falls, but on the other hand, his department hadn't grown. The tourist business was putting a strain on his officers. But that was a problem for another day.

It wasn't until they reached the kitchen that Belle said, "They went all through here."

He had to admit that this crime was strange. So far, they stole a puppy, and now they'd rifled through the kitchen. It didn't make sense, unless it was a diversion to throw them off the track of what they were really after.

Ding.

Ding. Ding.

When Belle pulled her phone out of her coat, he asked, "Do you need to get that?"

She looked at the screen and shook her head. "It's just my friends. They heard something was going on and wanted to make sure I was all right."

He was glad she had such good friends. "Maybe you should message them back."

Belle nodded. She typed a very brief message and then put the phone back into her pocket.

He turned his thoughts back to the crime scene. They were missing something. Perhaps the answer would be upstairs in one of the bedrooms.

He cleared his throat. "I take it you don't normally leave the cabinet doors hanging open?" He didn't think so, but he had to ask.

"No." Her answer was firm.

"Can you tell us if anything is missing?"

She walked over to the cabinets and hunched down. "The bag of puppy kibble is still here. So are the cans of moist dog food."

He watched as the color drained from her face. He figured she was panicking. And he couldn't blame her. Having someone break into her home—her safe zone—would rattle anyone.

"I can't believe someone did this." And then her eyes widened. "Do you think they'll hurt him?"

He saw a tear roll down her cheek and heard the waver in her voice. He acted on instinct and pulled her into his arms. He didn't know how she'd react. For all he knew, she might shove him away, yell at him or stomp off.

But she didn't do any of those things. Instead, she followed the lead of his pull until her head was resting against his shoulder. His arms tightened around her waist. And in that moment, he noticed how well they fit together—as though they were made for each other.

The last thought startled him to the core. His immediate instinct would be to step away from her because their connection was short-circuiting his mind. He fought that reaction. This moment wasn't about him or his totally out of control thoughts. This was about Belle.

Her home—her sanctuary—had been invaded. The puppy she obviously loved had been taken. And she was feeling off-kilter and longing for her four-footed friend. Giving her a hug was the least he could do in that moment.

He stood perfectly still with her in his arms. When he inhaled, the gentle scent of jasmine came over him. The scent was sweet and slightly musky. It was a complex scent, much like the woman in his arms.

She could be so frustrating and argumentative one moment, and then it was like the layers were peeled back to reveal her tender, caring side. And he wasn't sure how to deal with this gentler side of her.

He breathed in another whiff of jasmine. He didn't think he'd ever smell it again without recalling this moment—of having his arms wrapped around Belle.

She pulled away, and the moment was over as fast as it had started. She lowered her head and sniffed as she swiped at her eyes. "I'm sorry about that."

What was he supposed to say in response? Did he tell her he didn't mind her leaning on his shoulder? *No.* He didn't want her to get the wrong impression. He wasn't interested in her romantically.

She was simply a victim whom he was going to do his best to help.

Speaking of the case, they needed to get back to it. He had her look around the downstairs another time before he followed her upstairs. When they reached her bedroom, he hesitated. Even though he was working on a case, it always felt as though he were intruding when he went into a victim's bedroom.

Still, he stepped through the doorway. The walls were... He stopped and stared at them for a moment. They were the lightest shade of pink. *Weren't they?*

A white chest of drawers was over in the corner. There was a box on top of it, perhaps a jewelry box. The bedside tables had lamps on them. The queen-size bed frame matched the rest of the furniture. There was a white duvet with a red rose pattern.

The part that he hadn't anticipated was the mess. There were discarded clothes tossed across the bottom of the bed, as though she'd gotten up that morning and hadn't been sure what to wear. So she'd tried on and discarded outfit after outfit until she found the right one.

On the floor beneath the discarded clothes were various shades of high heels lying on their sides—again she couldn't make up her mind about what to wear. Closer to the closet, he noticed a pair of black knee-high boots also discarded. It seemed that Belle wasn't a decisive person—unless it came to him. She'd definitely made her mind up about him, and it was not positive.

"They've been through all of my drawers." Belle's voice drew him from his thoughts.

"Are you sure?" After all, the room wasn't the neatest.

"Of course, I am." She frowned at him.

"Don't touch them. Let me see if they checked them for fingerprints." He contacted his deputies who were still outside. They'd found footprints and tracks that looked like they belonged to an ATV as well as a partially open window with the latch broken.

After he finished his conversation with the deputies, he turned to Belle. "We should go downstairs."

"What's going on?" she asked.

"I'll tell you downstairs."

"No. I want you to tell me now." She pressed her hands to her rounded hips.

"Fine. They found footprints and tracks that most likely belong to an ATV." He didn't know what sort of reaction to expect from her. To his surprise, she appeared to take it in stride.

"Any sign of Odie?"

He sighed and rubbed the back of his neck. "I'm afraid not. Let's go downstairs until they have a chance to print this room."

He stood off to the side of the doorway in order for her to take the lead. However, he must not have stepped far enough out of the way because her shoulder brushed against him. And then he got another intoxicating whiff of her jasmine scent.

How had he ignored her beauty all of this time? Maybe it was that they'd been sparring with each other for so long he never took the time to see her in any other way.

And now wasn't the time to see her as a beautiful, desirable woman. Right now, he needed to stay focused on this break-in and the dognapping. He never had a case quite like this one.

As they made their way downstairs, questions came to him. "Do you know who is overly fond of your dog?"

"No."

"Maybe a family member? Or friend?"

At the bottom of the steps, she came to a halt and turned on him. Her fine brows were drawn together in a formidable look. "I don't have any close family. And none of my friends would have done it either."

Her frown didn't intimidate him, but he was relieved to see the fire come back to her eyes. "So, you believe whoever broke in here is a stranger to you?"

"Yes, I do."

He was willing to go along with this thinking to a certain point. Because his training dictated that he started with her inner circle and worked his way outward. However, he didn't want the conversation to stop now that he'd gotten her to start talking.

"If it was a stranger, what do you think they wanted?"

She looked at him like he'd lost his mind. "My dog."

He nodded. "I understand that, but they wanted something more. They wouldn't have searched your house if all they wanted was the dog. Think. Is there something valuable you have?"

The stubborn frown remained on her face. "Trust me. There's nothing valuable in this house."

"There has to be something here for them to break in. What do you know about the dog?"

Her brows rose. "Are you thinking that the original owner wanted him back?"

Parker shrugged. "I don't know. I'm just throwing around ideas."

"I don't know the dog's history. He came from Ohio as a stray."

Suddenly, he realized what was going on with the dog. "Is he one of the strays that Candi brought to town?"

Belle nodded. "Yes. But it was Merry Kringle that matched me with Odie. At the time, I didn't even want a pet until I met him. We instantly bonded. And now..." Her voice cracked with emotion. "I just don't understand why anyone would take him."

He made a note to speak to Candi Goodman and Merry Kringle. Maybe they could tell him more about Odie.

"Don't worry. We'll get to the bottom of this." He didn't usually make promises when he had absolutely no idea how he would resolve the issue, but there was something about Belle that had his mouth offering a promise he didn't know if he could deliver.

It took a while longer for the deputies to print the upstairs. In the meantime, Belle went through the downstairs to see if she could uncover anything that was missing. Aside from Odie, everything appeared to be there. Maybe it was something small, and it would take her a bit of time to notice it was missing.

Chapter Six

He was gone.

A roar of emotions churned within her.

The most dominant emotion was fear—fear for Odie's safety.

Belle couldn't believe someone had taken her puppy. It just didn't make any sense for anyone to break into her house and take her dog. Did someone hate her that much?

Now that the police had finished collecting clues, and everyone had left, Belle set about straightening up the house. She needed something to do. She couldn't sit still. And so, she tried to erase any sign of this awful evening, but try as she might, every time her gaze strayed across one of Odie's toys or his blanket, it all came rushing back to her.

She needed to be doing something to help find him. But where did she start? She didn't have a clue why he was taken. Maybe she could start calling people. Yes. That was a good idea. If news of Odie's kidnapping got out, the townspeople could help keep an eye out for him.

She grabbed her phone and was about to call Merry Kringle when she heard a knock at the door. Who would that be? She wasn't expecting anyone.

Then her body tensed. What if it was the dognapper? As soon as the thought passed through her mind, she realized how ridiculous it would be for a criminal to come knocking on her door. Still, she was hesitant to answer the door.

Knock-knock.

"Belle, it's Parker!"

She expelled a pent-up breath. She moved to the door and unlocked it. She peered out at him. "I thought you left."

"I did momentarily. Can I come in?"

"Oh. Sure." She opened the door wider. Once he was inside, she closed it against the frigid night air. Then she turned to him. "Did you forget something?"

"No. I'm staying." In his hand was a dark duffel bag.

"Staying?" It took her jumbled mind a minute to figure out what he'd meant. "You mean here?"

"I do."

She struggled not to gasp. They were, well...she wouldn't exactly call them enemies, but they certainly weren't friends. "But why? I mean, I'm fine."

His gaze searched hers. "Someone broke into your house this evening. This isn't something that happens in Kringle Falls." He frowned. "It doesn't help that you have a broken latch on a back window that they could come through again if they wanted. I'm not saying this to scare you. I just want you to realize that my concerns are legitimate."

She opened her mouth to argue with him, but before the words crossed her lips, she realized whether she liked it or not, he was right. She wordlessly closed her mouth. She couldn't believe the man who'd been writing her tickets regularly wanted to stay in her home.

"Maybe one of your deputies could keep an eye on things." Still not comfortable with the idea, she said, "Maybe one of your deputies could do increased patrols."

A small smile played at the corner of his mouth as he dropped his bag to the floor. He slipped off his coat, and then he took off his boots. He moved into the living room. He paused next to the Christmas tree, which wasn't much taller than he was. Parker looked right at home as he stood there in her living room in a navy-blue sweatshirt, jeans, and his stockinged feet.

His gaze lifted and met hers. "You sound like you don't want me around. Should my feelings be hurt?"

Was that a teasing tone in his voice? As a little smile played at the corners of his mouth, she realized he was just having a little fun. *So, he isn't a total grouch. Interesting.*

She tried again. "Don't you have work to do?"

He shook his head. "I have the night off. So, I'm all yours."

Belle stifled a gasp as her heart skipped a beat. *All hers?* Surely, he hadn't meant those words the way they sounded to her ears.

She also got the feeling he wasn't going anywhere. She didn't know how she felt about that. This whole evening had her struggling to keep up with the unexpected.

She crossed her arms and looked at him. "Is there anything I can say to change your mind?"

"No."

She was too tired to argue with him. "Fine. I'll make up the guest room."

"That won't be necessary."

Her eyes widened. "Why is that?"

"Because I'll sleep right here on the couch."

Her gaze moved from him to the couch, with its lumpy cushions, before returning back to him. "Trust me, you'll be more comfortable in a guest room."

"I don't doubt you're right, but I'm not here to get a good night's sleep. I'm here to protect you. I want to be down here where I can stop anyone who breaks in."

It had been a long evening, and she was too tired to argue with him. "I'll get you a pillow and a blanket."

As she walked away, she didn't know how she felt about having the sheriff under her roof. Knowing her luck, he'd find something else to ticket her for, but she couldn't even begin to know what it might be. Besides, the tickets were the least of her worries. She just wanted to know where Odie was and if he was okay.

She grabbed a blanket from the linen closet and a pillow from the guest bed. When she ventured back downstairs, Parker was no longer in the living room. She wondered where he'd gone. Maybe he came to his senses and left.

Then she heard a noise in the dining room. "Parker?"

"Yeah, it's me." He appeared in the doorway. "I was checking the other windows to make sure they were secure."

"And were they?" When he nodded, she said, "I'm going to make some phone calls to let people in town know that Odie is missing. Maybe someone has seen him." She doubted it because she was sure one of her friends would have already contacted her, but it was worth the effort. She just couldn't sit around here doing nothing.

"Have you eaten dinner?" he asked.

She shook her head. She didn't have a chance before her evening went totally off the rails. "I don't really have an appetite."

"Are you sure?" His concerned gaze searched hers.

She nodded. "But feel free to help yourself to anything in the kitchen. I'm just going to go upstairs and make those calls."

When she reached the steps, she paused to glance back toward the kitchen. She couldn't see Parker, but she could see the refrigerator door was open. It was so odd to have him in her house and she hated that it made her feel better to have him there. All she wanted was to wake up from this nightmare and find Odie next to her.

Her gaze moved to Odie's spot on the couch. It was so sad to see it empty. Tears burned the back of her eyes. She blinked repeatedly. She wasn't going to fall apart again.

She had work to do. She was going to make sure that everyone in Kringle Falls knew her furbaby was missing. Hopefully, someone would have a lead for her to follow.

As she started up the stairs, she heard what sounded like the clanging of pans coming from the kitchen. Apparently Parker had taken her at her word when she'd told him to help himself. She wondered what he was making. She was tempted to turn around and go investigate, but her concern for Odie kept her moving toward her bedroom. She'd check in on Parker later.

For living alone, the kitchen was well-stocked.

Parker stood in front of the stove, stirring the red sauce he'd made to go with the rotini pasta he'd just drained, oiled, and set aside. He'd made a marinara sauce because he couldn't find any meat to put in it. That was fine with him. He loved marinara. Now he had to hope that Belle liked it too. She might not have an appetite, but she needed to eat something.

He reached for a spoon and then tasted the sauce. Not too bad if he did say so himself.

Buzz.

He reached for his phone, which had been unusually quiet for a Friday night. When he checked the caller ID, he saw it was Deputy Paula Stark. He pressed the phone to his ear. "What have you got?"

"Aside from Belle's fingerprints, we have one other set. I ran them through the database but didn't get any hits. So, either this person never committed a B&E before, or this is the first time they left prints."

He thought about it for a moment. "I'm thinking this was their first. It certainly didn't seem like a sophisticated crime."

"Agreed."

"Anything else?" Parker braced himself for more problems.

"No. It's a quiet Friday evening."

After Parker ended the call. He served up two plates of food and carried them to the kitchen table. He moved to call up the stairs for Belle to join him when he heard her footsteps. He glanced up the stairs to find that she'd changed into black leggings and an over-sized gray sweatshirt with Santa on the front.

She rushed down the stairs. "I've got news."

"Why don't you sit down with me? You can tell me what you learned over dinner." He started toward the kitchen.

She followed him. "You made us pasta?"

He nodded. "Come on." He moved to the table and pulled out a chair for her. "Have a seat."

She hesitated. A frown settled over her face. Perhaps she didn't like the pasta. He was about to tell her she wouldn't hurt his feelings if she didn't like it. But before he could vocalize his thoughts, she took a seat.

After he sat across from her, she said, "I made some phone calls—okay, a lot of phone calls."

"So, what did you learn?" He hoped that she'd uncovered a thread they could pull on and see where it led them.

She picked up her napkin and spread it on her lap. "When I phoned Candi to see if she noticed anything because you know that she's been staying at your brother's place just down the road a little way." When Parker nodded in understanding, she continued. "Candi said that she stopped by around five. She wanted to see if we could have a pup date." When he sent her a confused look, she said, "You know a puppy playdate. Anyway, she noticed some of the lights were on. That's why she stopped. She thought I got home early from work. She knocked on the door, but after a while, she gave up when there was no answer. She said the strange part was when she got back in her car, the lights were suddenly off."

"That's good information. It tells us that she interrupted the suspect. And what time did you get home?"

Belle paused as though to give it some thought. "I usually get home at seven minutes after five. But this evening you...uh, we, um, talked." He noticed how her cheeks took on a rosy hue. "So, it would have been closer to a quarter after."

He cleared his throat. "And you said it was quiet when you got here?"

Again, she stopped to consider her answer. Then she nodded. "Yes."

"So, no faint sounds of any vehicles, snowmobiles, or ATVs?"

She pursed her plump lips as she searched her memory. "No. I don't recall hearing anything."

"That must mean that once Candi left, they grabbed your dog and left as well. The question I keep coming back to is: did they come here for the express purpose of stealing your dog? Or was that an afterthought?"

"You think they came here for something else?"

"It makes sense. If they only wanted the dog, there was no reason for them to search your bedroom." He picked up his fork and took a bite of the pasta. It wasn't too bad, considering she didn't have any fresh garlic, and he'd had to use garlic powder. The same for the onion.

Belle nodded. As she appeared to consider what they'd discussed, she also picked up her fork and began to eat.

She took a bite of pasta and swallowed. "What do you think they came here for?"

"That's my question for you?" He glanced around. "Is there anything of great value in here?"

She shook her head. "I can't think of anything. It's not like I keep a lot of cash on hand, just some jars of change, but that's all."

"And all of your electronics are here? Televisions, computers, that kind of thing?"

She nodded. "There are only two televisions: one in the living room and the other in my bedroom. I have one laptop. Wait." She jumped to her feet and rushed upstairs.

She returned with a frown on her face. "It's here."

"Well, just give it some more thought. Maybe something will come to mind."

"I hope so." She took a bite of the pasta. After she swallowed, she said, "This is good. Like really good."

He let out a laugh at her astonishment. "Thanks."

"No. Thank you for making dinner. I really appreciate it."

This was the friendliest they'd been with each other in years. He wondered how long it would last. He had no idea, but he would enjoy the peace while it lasted.

And so they ate in silence. Each of them was lost in their own thoughts. He was trying to figure out a way to find the owner of those fingerprints, but so far he didn't have a plan.

After they finished eating, Parker started to clear the table, just like his mother had taught him and his siblings from an early age. Belle jumped up and helped him. As he carried the dirty dishes to the sink, he was relieved to find that Belle had a dishwasher.

Together, they cleaned up the kitchen. At last, they'd achieved a companionable silence. As he worked, he kept thinking about the motive for the break-in. Was there something on Belle's computer they wanted? He doubted it. She worked in a boutique. It wasn't like she had top-secret plans or anything. So, then, what were they after?

Chapter Seven

S HE COULDN'T SIT STILL.

Her thoughts were racing. Where was Odie? Later that evening after going to her room to get some distance from the handsome sheriff, Belle made more phone calls. She wasn't able to reach Merry Kringle, which she found odd.

She was hoping someone would provide her with another clue, but no one heard or saw anything. Every person she spoke to promised to call her if they thought of anything that would help find Odie.

Belle headed back downstairs. Parker was sitting on the couch working on his laptop. He glanced up. For a moment, their gazes connected, and her heartbeat sped up. She dismissed her reaction to him. She told herself that she was imagining it. There was no way he was attracted to her.

As though he, too, felt the awkwardness of the moment, he glanced away. "I like your tree."

She could have merely said thank you and continued on her way, but he was going above and beyond to help her, so she decided it was only right for her to make an effort too. She stepped closer to the unlit Christmas tree. It just didn't feel right to turn on the lights when Odie was... Well, when he could be anywhere. But he had a fondness for the Christmas tree and would lie near it a lot of the time.

"It's a special tree to me." After the words crossed her lips, Belle regretted them. She hadn't intended to get too personal with him, but it was too late to take the words back now.

"The ornaments look unique."

"They are." She couldn't really convey its specialness without plugging in the twinkle lights. She moved to the tree where she bent over to put the plug into the outlet. When the white lights came on, she straightened. "My great-grandmother started collecting ornaments. The pink and blue ones were hers." And then Belle pointed to a couple of crocheted angel ornaments. "Once upon a time they were white, but they've aged into more of an antique white."

"So the tree is like a history of your family?" he asked.

"I never thought of it that way, but yes." She turned her attention back to the tree. She liked the way he'd described it. "The beaded ornaments were made by my grandmother."

The colorful beads were in the shapes of bells, Christmas trees, snowmen, and many other shapes. Each one picked up the light and made the tree practically glow.

"And what about the white ones with the painted designs?" Parker continued to stare at the tree.

No one had ever taken such an interest in her Christmas tree. His genuine curiosity touched a spot deep within her. She chose not to give that too much thought.

She stepped forward and picked up one of them. She held it in her palm. "These were hand-painted by my mother."

He leaned in closer for a better look. "Your mother was very talented."

After he finished looking at it, Belle held it in front of her face for a better look. He was right. Her mother had taken the time to paint the finest details. It was what made them stand out.

After Belle placed the ornament back on the tree, she turned to him. When she found him staring at her, her heart skipped a beat. She told herself to keep it together and not get lost in his chocolate-brown eyes.

She swallowed hard, hoping when she spoke her voice sounded normal. "Can I get you anything?"

His gaze moved to the couch and then back to her. "I'm good."

Without another word, she headed for the kitchen. After washing her hands, she moved to the fridge and withdrew eggs and cream cheese. Next, she grabbed her largest mixing bowl. She continued gathering everything she would need to make cookies. She'd made them so often she had the ingredients memorized, but she didn't know the exact amount of each. She opened a drawer and withdrew her mother's handwritten recipe card.

It was times like these when she really missed her mother. She had loved to bake, and she'd taken time to teach Belle to bake when she was still a little girl. They were some of Belle's fondest memories.

She turned around and nearly jumped out of her skin. There in the doorway stood all six-plus feet of Parker staring at her. She pressed a hand to her pounding chest.

"I didn't hear you enter." She lowered her hand and moved to the kitchen island. "That stealthy maneuverer must come in handy with you being the sheriff and all."

A half smile came over his handsome face. "It does. But I hadn't intended to scare you. I heard a noise and wondered what you were up to."

"Oh. I didn't mean to disturb you." She bent over and retrieved the stand mixer from the cabinet.

"You didn't. What are you doing?" He propped himself against the door jamb.

She wondered how honest she should be with him. It wasn't like they were friends or anything. But as he continued to stare at her with an inquisitive look on his face, she sighed. "When something is bothering me, I either clean or bake."

His gaze moved across the items on the island. "I take it you're going with the baking. What are you making?"

"Christmas cookies. There's a party at the Kringles' house tomorrow night." She gestured to the festive invitation with red and green glitter hanging on the front of her fridge. "I agreed to bring stuff for the cookie table."

He nodded. "I heard it's always a big party."

They invited most of the townspeople. It was definitely the height of the holiday season. "You sound like you've never been to one of their parties."

"I haven't." He said it as a matter-of-fact.

No wonder she couldn't remember ever seeing him there. "I take it you don't like parties."

He shrugged. "Just never had a reason to go."

"Who needs a reason to go to a party? They're just for fun." She made sure to get a new dress each year just for this particular party. She glanced across at him. "What do you do for fun?"

"You mean besides ticket people?" When she gaped at him, he smiled. Not just one of his half-smiles. No. This was a big smile that made his big brown eyes twinkle. "I'm just joking."

"Not funny. Not funny at all." But she did like the way his smile smoothed his frown lines and made him look years younger.

In fact, when he smiled, he was downright gorgeous. The thought made the breath catch in her lungs. What was she doing having thoughts like that about Parker? He was not her type at all. He was Mr. By-The-Book, and she was more live and let live.

However, now she was curious to know more about him. "Seriously, what do you do for fun?"

He shrugged. "I watch football."

Hey, she watched football too. Wait. Did that mean they had something in common?

She jerked her thoughts back to the conversation. "Do you go to the games? And wear face paint?"

Parker rolled his eyes. "No. I sit at home on my couch and watch the game."

"Alone?"

He once more shrugged. "Most of the time."

She was starting to see what was the matter with him. "You need to get a life."

He frowned at her. "I do have a life."

"I mean a social life."

"I interact every day with the public. When I'm off-duty, I like some quiet time."

How could she argue with that? "Do you have any pets? Maybe a cat? Or a dog?" And then to lighten the conversation, she asked, "How about a little pot-bellied pig?"

"A pig?" He let out a laugh. "No, I don't have a pet pig or any other pets."

As soon as he laughed, a small smile pulled at her own lips. Just as quickly, she felt guilty for enjoying herself while Odie was missing. Maybe this conversation wasn't the best idea. She turned her attention back to baking.

While she worked, she expected Parker to go back to working on his laptop. Instead, he pulled out a stool at the island and sat down. "What can I do?"

His question caught her off guard. "What do you mean?"

"With the baking. I can help." He seemed perfectly serious.

She hadn't baked with anyone since her mother died. The thought brought a pang of grief to her heart. She thought of turning him down, but he'd turned the recipe card around and was reading it.

She looked at the mixing bowl and tried to remember what came next. And then she remembered. "You can add the vanilla."

He picked up the little bottle of flavoring. "How much?"

"Two teaspoons."

He looked around. "Where's the measuring spoon?"

"I don't use one. Just guesstimate it."

"What?" He sent her a confused look.

"You know, just pour a little like you would to fill a measuring spoon and then repeat it."

He shook his head. "I can't do that."

She pressed a hand to her hip. "Why not?"

"Because it won't be the right amount."

"It'll be close."

"But it won't be exact. Can you hand me a measuring spoon?" He held out a hand.

She thought of continuing the argument but realized there was no point. This was just one more example of why they'd never be any more than...what? Friends?

As she added ingredients to the mixing bowl, she tried to ignore him, but instead, she was aware of every little move he made. His nearness and undivided attention had her unable to recall the recipe from memory, so instead, she had to follow the recipe card step by step. Thankfully, her mother was detailed, so Belle just had to read and do what the recipe instructed.

When at last the cookie dough formed a smooth ball, she flattened it into a round disc. She wrapped it in plastic wrap before placing it in the freezer for a few minutes.

When she turned around, she saw him studying his phone. "Anything new about Odie?"

He glanced up. His gaze met hers, but he seemed lost in thought. It took him a moment before he said, "Uh. No. Nothing. I'm sorry."

"I've been going through it in my mind, trying to figure out who might do something like this, but I can't come up with anyone I know who would do something so horrible as to take Odie. He must be so scared and confused." Suddenly, her emotional turmoil came washing over her. She blinked repeatedly. She wasn't going to fall apart—not now—not in front of Parker.

He reached across the island and placed his hand over hers. His touch was warm as he gave her a squeeze. "Hang in there. This investigation is only just beginning."

Thunk!

Belle's chest tightened. *What was that?* Her worried gaze moved to Parker. He pulled his hand from hers and sat up straighter, as though he were listening for the sound.

Thunk!

There it was again. Maybe it was someone at the door. She walked around the island to head for the front door. But before she could exit the kitchen, Parker held his arm out stopping her.

"Wait here." His voice was low but firm.

Thunk!

"I'll go investigate." And then he walked away.

She was left alone in the kitchen, and suddenly, she was relieved Parker had insisted on sleeping on her couch. If the criminal came back to finish what he'd started earlier, she didn't want to have to face him alone.

As she waited in the kitchen, she listened. The thunking sound was intermittent, but it was still there. Not able to stand still any longer, she began pacing. When she thought she heard a different sound, she stopped and listened. Then she'd resume her pacing.

It felt like eternity had passed when Parker returned. His hair was windswept, and his cheeks and nose were pink tinged from the cold. "You don't have to worry. It's just the wind. It's picked up. A loose shutter was pounding against the side of the house. I did my best to secure it. Hopefully, it'll hold for the night."

"Thank you." She suddenly felt silly for thinking it was someone trying to get into her house...again.

Belle got the cookie dough from the freezer and tore off a piece. She placed it on a floured countertop and then returned the rest to the freezer. It was time to cut out some cookies. Her favorite part.

When she noticed Parker was leaving the kitchen, she asked, "Would you like to help me decorate the cookies?"

With his back to her, he hesitated.

When he didn't respond, she said, "Never mind. I've got it."

He turned to her and retraced his steps. "I'd like to. What do you want me to do?"

"You could get the colorful sprinkles out of the corner cabinet." She gestured to the right cabinet.

Without a word, he headed for the sink to wash up. A few moments later, he returned to the island with his hands full of decorations. She rolled out the cookies and worked the cookie cutters while he decorated each cookie. To her surprise, he was artistic. Then again, she realized that even after knowing him since they were kids, she actually didn't know that much about him.

As she pressed a snowman-shaped cutter into the soft dough, she asked, "Have you ever thought about moving away from Kringle Falls?"

He shook his head. "My whole family is here. And I know it probably sounds strange, but we're really close."

"It doesn't sound strange at all." She thought of her parents and wished they were still around. "It sounds really nice that you have that sort of relationship with them."

"What about you? Ever think of exploring the world?"

"Sometimes. Especially after my parents died. Everything about Kringle Falls reminds me of them. My mother loved Christmas. She loved living in a Christmas town."

"So, why didn't you leave?"

"I don't know if it was just one thing that kept me here. I think it was more like a bunch of things. Like my friends, the memories, and this house is just... Well, it's my home. I don't want to go searching for another place that gives me the same warm and cozy feelings that I get right here." And then realizing that perhaps she'd revealed more about herself than she'd intended, especially with the sheriff who made a point of ticketing her, she pressed her lips together.

Buzz.

He reached for his phone. "It's work."

"No, problem. I've got the rest of this." She glanced at the next two trays of cookies, which needed decorating. "They won't look as good as yours, but they'll have sprinkles on them."

He arched a brow. "Make 'em look pretty."

He turned and pressed the phone to his ear as he left the room. "Bishop."

She was touched that he'd taken time to keep her company. He didn't have to do it. The more time she spent with him the more she found herself liking the man she couldn't stand the day before.

What was she supposed to make of him? Which one was he? The grumpy, strict sheriff or the man who made her smile and took time to talk to her?

If Odie were here, he'd let her know his thoughts about Parker. Odie had a good sense of people. And she missed him so much.

"I'll get you back," she whispered into the night, hoping her pup sensed how much she loved and missed him.

Chapter Eight

It was a long night.

There was a lot of tossing and turning. Once Belle finally fell asleep, she'd slept deeply. There was no energy for dreams. She wouldn't have slept that soundly if it weren't for Parker. And it bothered her that he could make her feel secure in her own home. She'd always prided herself on being able to take care of herself.

Saturday morning, she'd slept later than she'd wanted. She rushed through her shower and dressed. As she applied her makeup and pulled her hair back into a ponytail, she realized Parker most likely had already left, and she... Well, she would figure out some way to find Odie. There was no way her puppy disappeared without a trace.

And then a thought came to her: she'd stop by Purr 'n Woof. Someone who steals a dog would need some puppy food. With the thought in mind, she soundlessly rushed to the stairs.

When she reached the first floor it surprised her to find Parker on the couch working on his laptop. He was wearing gray sweatpants with a long-sleeved T-shirt. His stockinged feet were resting on the coffee table. His hair was mussed up, as though he'd dragged his fingers through it many times. She wondered what he was working so intently on.

"I didn't think you'd still be here," she said.

He briefly glanced over his laptop at her before returning his attention to his computer. "Trying to get rid of me?"

Maybe. "I just thought you'd have to work."

He continued to type something. Without looking up, he said, "I'm off this weekend, so I'm all yours."

Wait. Is he serious? No. Her heart beat faster. She didn't know if her body's reaction was good or bad. "Well, I'm headed out as soon as I get some coffee."

"Mind if I grab a quick shower?"

"Uh. No. Not at all. The bathroom is at the top of the steps. There are towels in the closet. And I even saved you some hot water."

"That was mighty kind of you. I won't be long."

He closed his laptop and set it on the coffee table. He got to his feet, grabbed his duffel bag from next to the couch, and headed upstairs.

Wordlessly, she turned and headed for the kitchen. She glanced at the clock on the wall and realized the pet store didn't open for another twenty-one minutes. She sighed. So much for her quick escape.

She moved to the kitchen counter. She grabbed a red cup from the cabinet and placed it on the coffeemaker. After filling the reservoir with fresh water, she dropped in a new pod and started the coffeemaker. Then out of habit, she moved to the fridge and reached for the dog food. With the food in hand, she straightened. It was then she realized she was about to feed Odie—her sweet puppy who was no longer there.

With a groan, she returned the food to the fridge. Her stomach growled a complaint. While she had the door open, she glanced around at the various food items, but she didn't have much of an appetite. All her stomach needed was some coffee. Instead, she grabbed the creamer from the fridge door and then closed it.

She'd just finished fixing her to-go coffee cup and took a big gulp, when Parker entered the kitchen. His hair was still damp from his very quick shower. He wore a navy-blue T-shirt with the sheriff's office logo on the left chest. The sleeves hugged his muscled biceps while the shirt struggled to cover his broad shoulders. She swallowed hard.

Catching herself staring, she turned her attention to putting the creamer back in the fridge. The coolness of the fridge washed over her heated face. She took her time glancing around the shelves.

When she at last straightened and turned, she said, "Well, I should get going."

He arched a brow. "Aren't you going to eat?"

"Maybe I already ate. You don't know." She drank some more of her coffee.

"I'm a sheriff, remember? I'm trained to be observant." He nodded toward the sink. "There are no dirty dishes. No crumbs on any of the counters. And your stomach is rumbling."

The heat rushed back to her cheeks. She didn't know he could hear it. "I'll be fine. I'll, uh...grab something in town." She started out of the kitchen, then stopped and turned back to him. "Thank you for dinner and for helping with Odie..."

She couldn't bring herself to thank him for sleeping on her couch. It would make her seem weak, like she couldn't take care of herself. And she could. She'd done just that since her parents died. Yet, last night when she'd drifted off to sleep, she'd slept soundly because she didn't have to worry about anyone coming back to finish the job they'd started.

"You're welcome. Should I just lock up when I leave?"

She nodded. "Yes." And then her gaze met his. "Will you call me as soon as you learn anything about Odie?"

"I will. I have calls out to neighboring towns."

She didn't want to think about the fact that Odie could be anywhere by now. Why would someone take him? She didn't understand. It wasn't like he was a purebred or anything.

She continued to mull over the different scenarios as she put on her coat and boots. She opened the front door and gasped.

Immediately, Parker was by her side. "What's wrong?"

She pointed to a piece of paper taped to the door.

As she reached out for it, Parker pulled her arm away from it. "Don't touch it. It could have prints or something that will lead us to Odie."

She continued to stare at the note. Her gaze took in the block letters:

We have your dog. Don't do anything stupid. We're watching you. If you want your dog back, go to the Christmas party tonight. More instructions to follow.

Belle was grateful she hadn't taken time to eat that morning because suddenly, the coffee in her stomach took a nauseous lurch. She turned on her heel and raced up the stairs to the bathroom.

"Belle?" Concern rang out in his voice.

Thankfully, he had the decency not to follow her. When she returned, Parker was just finishing up a phone call. He turned to her. His eyes shone with worry. "Are you okay?"

She was embarrassed that she'd gotten so worked up it had made her sick. "Do you think the note will help you find Odie?"

"I don't know. But it bothers me that whoever did this is was so bold that they came to the front door while I was here."

She didn't like it either. Just the thought sent goosebumps cascading down her arms. "Do you think they're out there?" She moved to the window. "Watching us?"

It made her angry that some deranged person was out there with her dog and disrupting not only her life but Parker's life too. She was intent on stopping them, but she wasn't sure how to do it yet.

"I have to go," she said.

When she moved to walk out the door, Parker stepped in her way. "You aren't going anywhere alone."

She sighed. "What? You aren't going to follow me around. Don't you have things you should be doing?"

He stepped closer to her and stared deep into her eyes. "Belle, you can't take any chances with this person. You have no idea what they want with you or what they're capable of."

"Well, if their intent was to scare me, they're doing a good job." She quickly pressed her lips together.

She couldn't believe she'd admitted that to him. It was just the shock of learning the dognapper had been back to her house that had her speaking without filtering her words.

"You don't have to be scared as long as I'm around. This is what I've trained for."

She shook her head. Hoping to smooth things out, she said, "I can take care of myself. Besides, what's going to happen? I'm going into town in broad daylight. There will be plenty of people around. I'll be safe."

He arched a brow as he frowned at her. "Has anyone told you that you're stubborn?"

She smiled and nodded. "My mother. Many times."

She turned and opened the front door. She heard some shuffling behind her, but she didn't glance back.

"Okay. Let's go." Parker's voice came from right behind her.

When she stopped, he ran into her. She spun around. "What are you doing?"

"I need to go to town, so we might as well go together. I'll drive." He said it as though she was just supposed to be all right with him escorting her around.

They lived in a small town. If she was to arrive in the middle of town with him, tongues would be wagging before she even stepped foot out of the vehicle. Parker was the very last man she wanted to be romantically linked to.

"I can drive myself," she said in a firm voice.

"Okay. I'll ride with you."

She restrained a frustrated sigh. She wasn't going to let him see just how much he was getting on her nerves. In the calmest voice she could muster, she said, "How do you know I'm going where you need to go?"

He shrugged. "It's Kringle Falls. Every place is walkable."

Her back teeth ground together. Now she remembered why they hadn't gotten along all of these years. She might be stubborn, but he was definitely next level.

Still, she didn't have time to argue with him. Every minute she spent verbally dueling with him was another minute that Odie was missing. "Fine," she said, "let's go."

"Go and start the car. I'm going to make sure the house is secure."

When she stepped outside, she found the sidewalk shoveled, and the snow had been cleaned off her car. When had he done all of that?

She moved to the car and started it. When she glanced over at the passenger seat, the napkins were still sitting there. She opened the glove box and shoved them inside.

The only thing left on the seat was the latest ticket he'd written her. She picked it up and looked at it. It was only then she realized he hadn't fined her. He'd given her a warning. *A warning*.

She slipped the piece of paper into her bag. A little smile tugged at the corners of her lips. Maybe there was hope for Parker after all.

When Parker got into the car, he looked at her and asked, "What are you smiling about?"

She was still smiling? She stopped, hoping she now had a neutral expression. As she glanced over at him, he seemed so close. With him next to her, her Jeep suddenly seemed to shrink. His broad shoulders were practically brushing hers. And her heart was thumping against her ribs.

Agreeing to let him ride with her to town was a mistake. A big mistake.

But it was too late to back out of this now. She started the engine and then put the vehicle in reverse. She was nervous as she maneuvered her way along the icy roadway. Luckily, she didn't have far to go.

At last, she turned onto Main Street. Her pulse was racing. Having Parker in the passenger seat, watching everything she did, was like being a teenager again and taking her driving test.

"You know you can go the speed limit," Parker said.

She glanced down at the dashboard. He was right. She was five miles an hour below the speed limit. It was his fault. He was making her nervous.

Not wanting him to know just how much his presence was getting to her, she said, "The roads are slick."

He didn't say anything. And then a low "Mm...hmm..." reached her ears.

Her back teeth once more ground together. It was time for him to go back to his life and leave hers alone. "I don't need you to follow me around."

"I'm not. We just happened to be going in the same direction."

She didn't buy it. She'd seen the deep frown on his handsome face when she'd found the note on the front door. Was he that concerned about her safety? Or was his ego pricked that someone had the audacity to sneak onto her porch, and he didn't have a clue they'd been there?

"Uh-huh." She didn't believe him. "And what do you need in town?"

"Security cameras."

This was news to her. "And where exactly are you planning to install these cameras?"

"All around the perimeter of your house."

She shook her head. "No."

"What do you mean no?" His voice rumbled with agitation. "You have some criminal lurking around your place. You have to take precautions. I can't be at your place twenty-four seven."

"You're right. You need to leave as soon as we get back, and you can take your cameras with you." She knew she was being obstinate, but at the moment everything felt as though it were spinning out of her control.

"Belle, you're being unreasonable. We have no idea what this person is capable of."

She needed to reclaim a modicum of control over her life, which had been invaded first by some criminal and then by this well-meaning but intrusive sheriff. She drew in a deep breath and slowly released it. But she realized this person could be dangerous, and with the cameras, Parker wouldn't need to sleep on her couch. "Fine. Install your cameras."

"Okay." He didn't have any little digs for her.

She parallel parked a little way down the road from the pet shop. "How long will you be?"

He arched a brow and smiled. "Why? Are you planning to leave me behind?"

Just that little bit of smile and his teasing tone broke the tension that was coursing through her body. In turn, she smiled when she said, "Don't think it hasn't crossed my mind."

"I shouldn't be more than a half hour. How about you?"

"I don't know. I want to talk to some people about Odie. I want everyone in this town to know that he's missing. I need everyone keeping an eye out for him. I need all the help I can get."

"Even mine?" His tone this time was totally serious.

She sighed. "Even your help."

"Then I best get to it." He opened the Jeep door and got out.

As she made her way along the sidewalk, a light snow began to fall. Just what they needed, more snow to add to the several inches of snow they already had on the ground. Still, she couldn't deny that it gave Kringle Falls Christmas vibes. Between all of the white stuff and the various shops along Main Street painted in shades of red, green, and white, this place was rocking the holidays. She supposed that was why they were known as a Christmas town.

She glanced up and spotted the white wooden sign hanging in front of the pet store. Painted in black letters it read: *Purr 'n Woof Supplies*. This was her destination.

She pushed open the glass door and heard the familiar sound of jingle bells. There was a silver jingle bell tree hanging on the door.

She glanced around the front of the store. There was no one at the checkout counter. There had to be someone there. "Hello?"

Belle walked past the displays of pet toys and snacks. In the middle of the shop were aisles of pet food, squeaky toys, and any other item you might need for your furbaby. There was no one there either.

In the back was a fenced-off training area. She'd always thought after the holidays that she would bring Odie, and they could take a class together. The thought brought a pain to her heart as tears burned the backs of her eyes. She blinked repeatedly as she struggled to get her emotions under control.

She swallowed hard and hoped her voice didn't betray her roller-coaster emotions. "Hello?"

"Good morning." Merry Kringle stepped out of the office and approached her with a warm smile on her face.

Merry was an older woman with short curly snow-white hair. She had blue eyes that twinkled when she laughed. She wore gold wire-rimmed glasses. Her cheeks were rosy, and her lips were upturned with one of her warm smiles.

When Belle was young, she was certain Merry was, in fact, Mrs. Claus. Who could blame a child for having those thoughts? The woman could easily play the part without any effort. And of course, there was the fact that her husband, Kris Kringle, looked just like Santa with his white beard and round belly.

And today, like most other days, Merry was wearing a red dress and white apron. It only perpetuated the idea that she was Santa's wife. Sometimes, Belle wondered if there was something Merry wasn't sharing with them—was she really Mrs. Claus? The ridiculous thought had a smile tugging at her lips.

Merry glanced around, as though she had lost something or someone. And then her attention centered on Belle. "Where's Odie?"

"You haven't heard?"

Merry's brows drew together as the smile faded from her face. "We were out of town last night. Did something happen?"

"I tried to call you last night, but it went to voicemail."

"Sorry. I didn't have my charger cord with me. What's going on?"

Belle rehashed what had happened over the past twenty-four hours. "And that's why I'm here. I needed to know if you've seen any strangers buying dog food or anything that would make you suspicious." Realizing that she was grasping at straws, she said, "I'm desperate. I don't know what to do to get him back."

"Of course you're worried. I can't believe anyone from Kringle Falls would do something so horrible."

"I agree. But they have to live close by because there was a note on my front door this morning. They said they're watching me." A chill raced down her spine.

Merry's eyes widened. "That's concerning. You mean they were on your front porch while you were sleeping?"

She nodded.

"That's scary. What's the sheriff doing about it?"

"Everything he can." Even though they didn't always get along, he had been there for her since Odie had been dognapped, and she appreciated it. "He slept on my couch last night in case they came back."

Merry's eyes momentarily widened, and then a smile bloomed on her face.

Belle sighed. "It's not like that, so don't go there. He was just doing his job."

"His job, huh? I can't recall him sleeping on anyone else's couch."

"No other Kringle Falls resident had their dog kidnapped."

Jingle-jingle.

They both turned toward the front of the store. In walked Mary Johnson and her husband, Josh. They had their dog, Scout, a black lab.

"Excuse me," Merry said. "I'll be back."

Belle watched as Merry moved toward the couple and extended one of her sunny greetings. Belle wasn't sure what to do now. Merry wasn't any help, and she was really counting on Merry knowing something. Merry always had her ear to ground and knew what was going on with most everyone in town.

Then again, Merry had mentioned being out of town. That might have something to do with Merry's lack of knowledge. Or maybe Merry was right, and whoever took Odie wasn't from Kringle Falls. If that were the case, how were they ever supposed to find Odie?

Her thoughts returned to the note on the front door. Why did they want her to go to the party that evening? Were they going to be there? She doubted it. They would know that she intended to have them arrested. So, then what was the point?

Chapter Nine

SOMETIMES DUTY REQUIRED SACRIFICE.

Parker had spent the afternoon installing surveillance cameras around Belle's house. She had been resistant to the idea, but she agreed as long as he was willing to take them back down once Odie was found and the dognapper was arrested.

It was time to go to the Christmas party at the Kringles' house. It was an annual event and one that Parker did his best to avoid at all costs. Usually, he opted to work the weekend of the party, but this year the scheduling hadn't worked out for him. Although, with Belle in a spot, he supposed the scheduling worked out for the best.

And so, now it was his duty as the sheriff of Kringle Falls to protect the town's citizens. And though he'd normally assign one of his deputies to handle this task, this was the woman who he'd had a crush on in high school. He didn't want to examine too closely his motivations for providing round-the-clock protection.

For better or worse, he was escorting her to the party. He had a bad feeling that the suspect hadn't found whatever it was that they had been searching for, and they were moving on to Plan B. And that had him on alert. For all he knew, it could be an ex of Belle's. Although, his deputies had interviewed the men from Belle's recent past, and they all had alibis.

He had been surprised that in the past couple of years, none of her romantic relationships had worked out. He had no doubts that Belle had been the one to end those relationships. Any man who was fortunate to date her, wouldn't let her go.

The thought stopped him in his tracks. Did he really think Belle was such a catch? If he let himself look beyond her habit of breaking the law, he had to admit she was the most beautiful woman he'd ever known. She baked a tasty cookie. And she wasn't so bad to talk to. In fact, he enjoyed talking to her. There were a lot of other great qualities about her, but he refused to go there. He was there on a job, nothing more. When it was over, they'd go back to ignoring each other.

He'd do well to keep his focus on the case. Everything they'd uncovered led him to believe the suspect hadn't broken into her house for the dog. There was something more afoot, and until he figured that out, he was keeping a close eye on Belle.

That morning, after he'd bought the security cameras, he'd had Belle stop by his apartment. He'd picked up a few things, including some clothes for the party. He didn't want to go to the party, but he didn't trust anyone else to watch over Belle.

He didn't know what to expect after she'd received that note. They hadn't hinted if they'd be at the party, which he doubted. He hated that they were always one step ahead of him. He didn't like any part of this dognapping.

Footsteps sounded on the staircase, drawing his attention. He glanced up from where he'd been sitting on the couch. The first thing he saw were silver heels and then long bare legs. He swallowed hard.

And then there was a red satin skirt that ended a couple of inches above her knees. The top portion of the dress was white with a fitted waist and cap sleeves. There was a red gemstone wreath pin on her chest.

She looked... *Wow! She is stunning.* If this was a real date, he would be tripping all over himself, trying to impress her. But this was work. It was absolutely nothing else.

He got to his feet as he continued to bask in her beauty. Belle had worn her hair down. The reddish-brown silky strands fell below her shoulders. In fact, he'd be willing to bet that her hair was down to the middle of her back. His hands tingled to reach out and run his finger through those silky strands. He resisted the urge.

She wore some makeup, but it didn't overpower her natural beauty. There was some mascara that accentuated her long lashes, which acted like a frame around her azure-blue eyes. And her plump lips were red and glossy, just perfect for kissing.

"Do you like it?" Her voice drew him from his wayward thoughts.

He wasn't sure how to answer her. Like which part in particular? Because he liked the full package. She was absolutely stunning. And the admission, even to just himself, was profound.

He swallowed hard again, hoping when he spoke, his voice sounded normal. He meant to tell her that she looked fine, but what came out was something a bit different. "You are so beautiful. You're going to have all of the men at the party staring at you."

Now what had he gone and said that for? It wasn't like this was a real date or anything. He was going to be on the job all evening, waiting for this dognapper to make contact.

Still, he noticed how his words caused her cheeks to take on a pink hue. How was it possible that her blushing made her even prettier?

Knowing he was headed down a dangerous path, he moved toward the door. He shrugged on his coat. Then he automatically grabbed hers. He'd meant to put on his coat and head out the door to warm up his pickup. Instead, he approached her at the foot of the steps and held her coat out for her to put on.

When she gave him a quick once-over, a frown creased her face. "Why are you dressed like that?"

He looked down at his navy-blue T-shirt paired with a navy-blue blazer and a pair of jeans. "What's wrong with it?" His gaze lowered to his footwear. "Don't you like the boots? I wasn't sure about those."

"No. I mean, yes, I like what you're wearing. And the boots go well. What I want to know is why you're dressed like you're going to the party?"

"Because I am." He sent her a smile. "I'm your escort."

Her eyes widened in surprise. "You think you're going on a date with me?" She pressed a hand to her chest. "What gave you that idea?"

Okay. So maybe he hadn't phrased his words correctly. But why did she have to act like a date with him was the worst idea she'd ever heard? His pride took a direct hit.

As she put on her coat, he tried again. "It's not a date. I'm going to protect you in case the dognapper tries to pull something tonight."

"So, you're going to be my bodyguard?" She arched a brow.

He wasn't sure how he felt being called a bodyguard—especially her bodyguard. Still, she didn't seem as opposed to a bodyguard versus a date. "Fine. I'll be your bodyguard."

She looked as though she was considering it. "But what about the house? Aren't you supposed to be guarding it."

He pulled his phone from his back pocket. He brought up the app that controlled the cameras he'd just installed. He turned his phone around so she could see the control panel with the various views of the house.

"You have my house on your phone?" She pressed her hands to her rounded hips as she leveled him with a disapproving gaze.

He averted his gaze. "Only until we catch this guy."

"And what if it's a girl?"

He closed the app. "What?"

"You keep calling the dognapper a guy, but what if it's a woman? You know crime is an equal opportunity profession."

Was she serious? He struggled not to roll his eyes. "Fine. It could be a man or woman. There. Are you happy?"

She smiled at him. "Yes, I am."

He had a feeling she was being difficult just to annoy him. Well, if that was her goal, then she'd succeeded. "Are you ready to go?"

"Are you still insisting on accompanying me? Even though the place is going to be filled with people we both know and trust."

"Yes, I am. And don't try to talk me out of it. You'll only be wasting your time."

"Fine. I have to get the tray of cookies in the kitchen and then we can go."

"I'll go start the pickup." He headed outside.

He could tell this was going to be a long evening, especially if Belle decided to argue every move with him. But if she thought anything she said would stop him from doing his job, she was wrong. He was going to keep her safe. And with a little bit of luck, he would bring her dog home to her in time for Christmas.

The party was in full-swing.

Belle didn't know how so many people fit into the Kringles' home. It was a large red Victorian house with white trim and a candle in every window. There were guests at every turn. It felt as though the whole town were there, but she knew that wasn't possible.

She really wished she could relax and enjoy herself, but between Parker dogging her every step and the anxiety of anticipating contact with the dognapper, she was wound tight. Nevertheless, Belle did her best to paste a smile on her face and speak the appropriate greetings.

Everyone had heard about Odie's abduction. There were hugs and words of comfort. She knew they all meant well, but it was a lot for her. She eventually excused herself and went to get a drink.

With a glass of punch in hand, Belle looked over the crowd of festively dressed friends and acquaintances. Christmas songs played in the background. And... She inhaled deeply. In the air was the scent of holiday potpourri with hints of cloves, allspice, citrus and evergreen.

She wondered if the dognapper was among them. The thought of Odie being stuck in some cage in a dark corner caused her smile to falter. Was he afraid? Was he wondering why she hadn't come for him?

She moved to a quiet corner while attempting to keep the tears at bay. There were a few curious looks here and there, but no one said anything to her. She did not want to fall apart at a party and ruin everyone else's evening. And yet she couldn't leave yet. The dognapper hadn't made contact yet.

"Hey, are you all right?" Parker's voice came from just behind her. It carried with it a caring tone that warmed a spot in her chest. He'd spoken so softly that no one around them appeared to have overheard.

When she turned to him, the concern shone in his brown eyes. She didn't trust her voice in that moment, so she nodded in response.

"I've made the rounds," Parker said. "I haven't seen any strangers."

"Are we sure they're actually going to show up?" She so desperately wanted to get Odie back and move past this nightmare.

Parker's gaze continued to surveil the room. "Your guess is as good as mine."

Then she had a thought. "Maybe if you aren't around, they'll approach me. I know you're out of uniform, but everyone here knows that you're the sheriff." When he didn't respond, she said, "Go. Make yourself scarce."

"I don't like it."

"And I don't like having Odie dognapped. We all have things we have to deal with." She wasn't going to back down. She needed to do whatever it took to get her puppy back. "Go. I'll be fine. I'm in a crowded room. What could possibly happen?"

"That's what worries me." He frowned at her. She leveled her shoulders and stared right back at him. "Fine." He sighed. "I'll go outside and check the perimeter. But if you need me, call me."

"I don't have your number." The words were out of her mouth before she could stop them. She wasn't going to need his number or him. She could take care of herself in a room full of friends.

He held his hand out to her. "Let's have it."

She knew he wanted her phone, and she only had herself to blame for this. She withdrew it from her small beaded handbag. When she went to hand it to him, their fingers touched. It felt as though she'd just been zapped by a bolt of static electricity. The sensation pulsed up her arm and settled in her chest, making her heart pound.

She yanked her hand back. What was that? She'd never felt anything like it before.

When he handed the phone back to her, she made sure their fingers didn't touch. Although, she was certain it wouldn't happen again. Still, she didn't want to take any chances.

She meandered through the party until she bumped into Candi. "Hi. Are you getting to know everyone?"

"It's taking me a little bit to put the names with faces." Candi sent her a concerned look. "How are you?"

Belle shrugged and lowered her voice. "I still have no idea who took Odie."

"I can't believe they broke into your house and took him. Who does that?"

"It's the question I keep asking myself." Not wanting to focus on her own problems, she changed the subject. "How are you and Michael doing?"

A big smile came over Candi's face. "We're doing really well." She leaned in closer and lowered her voice. "I didn't know I could be this happy. You should try it."

Distracted as she searched the partygoers for someone who stood out, she asked, "Try what? Being happy?"

"No. Falling in love." Candi's eyes twinkled with her bubbly happiness.

"Belle." Parker called from across the room. One look at his handsome face and she knew something bad had happened. Had they found Odie? Was he... She refused to finish that thought. It didn't stop her heart from sinking down to her high heels.

She turned to see the creases in his forehead and his brows drawn together. *Oh, no. This isn't going to be good.*

She turned back to Candi. "Sorry. Looks like Parker needs me." When Candi got a big grin on her face, Belle said, "Not that way."

Candi sighed. "You can't blame me for wishing."

Belle resisted the urge to roll her eyes. "We have nothing in common."

"Really?"

Before Belle could respond, Parker approached her. There was a distinct frown on his face as he handed over her coat. It was different from his usual scowl. The lines between his brows and bracketing his mouth were deeper.

"We have to go." He reached out to her, gripping her upper arm.

When he started to walk away with her in tow, she planted her feet. "Parker, stop."

When he turned back to her, she lowered her gaze to his hand on her arm. Immediately, he dropped his hand to his side. "Sorry. But we have to go."

"I'm not going anywhere until you explain what's going on." She crossed her arms as though bracing herself for the worst news.

"There's another break in at your place."

"Oh. Why didn't you say so?" Thank goodness it wasn't bad news about Odie. She shrugged on her coat as they moved toward the door. "Let's go."

She couldn't believe there was another break-in at her house. What did it mean? What did they want? The questions circled round and round in her mind. But the answer eluded her.

Chapter Ten

He refused to let anything happen to her.

Parker reached into his pocket for his pickup keys. His other hand reached out for her hand. When their fingers touched, he noticed the slight tremor in her hand. He couldn't blame her. It had to be unnerving to have someone intrude into your inner sanctum. Not once but twice.

It didn't matter how annoying she could be at times. He wouldn't let anything happen to her. It was more than just his job. There was something about Belle. Something in the way she cared about her puppy—about the way she cared about her friends and attended a Christmas party when he knew it was the last place she wanted to be, but she hoped her presence would help bring her puppy home safely.

He couldn't help but wonder if he got to know her better, what else he would admire about her. He halted his thoughts. He wasn't going to get to know her better. Once this case was over, they'd go their separate ways.

He opened the passenger side door for Belle. After she got in, he closed the door. He rushed around to the driver's side and jumped in. He started the pickup and pulled out.

"You turned the wrong way." There was an urgency in her voice.

"I didn't. This is the way to my parents' house."

"What?" Her voice rose. "We don't have time to go visiting. We have to find out why that man or woman was in my house again."

He slowed to a full stop at the intersection and put on the turn signal. "You're going to stay at my parents while I check things out at your place."

"No. Absolutely not." Her voice was firm with a note of restrained anger.

He still had a couple of blocks to convince her that accompanying him could be dangerous. His deputies were on the other side of town from her house. They were en route, but it was still going to take them ten minutes. He was closer but dealing with Belle was taking time.

He proceeded through the intersection and continued toward his parents' place. "You don't understand." His phone vibrated in his pocket. Every time there was movement detected in the house, his phone alerted him. "They are still in your house."

"Then turn around. Hurry up."

"No." He refused to put her in danger. The whole time he was trying to clear the house, he'd be thinking about her and that would be dangerous. "I can't do what I need to do if I'm worried about you."

She crossed her arms. "You don't have to worry about me. I can take care of myself."

He pulled to a stop in front of his parents' place. "Please, get out. My parents are expecting you." When she didn't budge, he said, "Belle, you're wasting time."

"Just go. I'll stay in the car."

He had a feeling this was the best deal he was going to get from her. Time was ticking, and his phone kept vibrating with alerts. "Do I have your word that you will stay in the car?"

There was a slight hesitation. "Yes. Go. Go!"

Just then his parents' front porch light came on. He'd have to explain it to them later. He stomped the accelerator. He waited for Belle to point out that he was speeding, but she was utterly silent. He had a feeling that if she were driving, she'd be doing the exact same thing.

A five-minute drive took him just under three minutes. When they pulled up, his deputies had already arrived. He didn't say a word as he jumped out of the pickup. He left the engine running so Belle wouldn't get cold.

He crouched down and pulled his backup gun from his ankle holster. Then he rushed toward the darkened house. A flash of light streaked across a window on the first floor. He wondered if it was from one of his deputies or if the suspect was still inside.

With his gun in hand, he stepped through the open front door. He paused and listened. He heard a couple of footsteps.

"Clear" came a female voice.

"Clear" came a male voice.

The familiar voices came from upstairs. So, then why did he hear some sort of shuffling coming from the living room?

Parker took quiet, sure steps toward the darkened living room. Luckily, it was a clear night. The moonlight shone through the windows, allowing him to see the outline of someone.

Parker's body flooded with adrenaline. He took quiet, measured steps. He glanced around to make sure there weren't any other intruders. He didn't see anyone else.

"Sheriff's Office!" He squinted into the dark with his hand on the gun. "Hands up."

The next thing he knew, something hard hit him in the side of the head. The unexpected impact made him see stars as he lost his balance. He went down hard.

When he regained his senses, he heard a jingling sound. Then something crashed to the floor. This was immediately followed by the shattering of glass. A frigid breeze smacked him in the face. Parker gave his head a shake before scrambling to his feet.

With his gun still in his other hand, he moved toward the suspect. "Stop. Police."

The dark shadow of a person escaped through the broken window. Parker rushed to the window. With each footstep, he felt something crunch beneath his feet. Whatever it was, it appeared to be all over the floor. He didn't have time to investigate. He had a criminal to catch.

The moment he reached the broken window, the bright overhead lights came on. He was momentarily blinded. At the same time, he heard a motor start, and then someone gunned it as they made their getaway. It sounded like a snowmobile. *Wait. No. An ATV.*

He squinted into the night. All he saw was the red glow of the taillights fading into the night. When his gaze lowered, he noticed blood on the broken shards of glass. *Gotcha!*

"Parker!" Belle's voice held a worried tone. Her beautiful blue eyes were rounded with fear. "You're bleeding."

"I am?" He raised his hand to his face and pressed it to the area that hurt. When he lowered his arm, he saw his fingertips were covered with bright red blood. That wasn't good.

"Boss, I'll call the ambulance." Deputy Luke Williams's voice held a shocked tone.

"No. The suspect went out the window. I think he took off on an ATV. See if you can track it."

"On it." Deputy Williams turned and jogged out the door.

Belle reached for her phone. "I'll call the ambulance."

"It's not necessary." Parker retraced his steps. When his head began to pound, and the room tilted to the side, he came to a stop. He closed his eyes and lifted his hand to his temple. He willed the pain to go away.

Belle stepped up to him. She reached out and touched his upper arm. She gave him a reassuring squeeze. "You need to sit down."

"Not here."

"The couch is right over there."

When his vision cleared, he said, "You can't be in here."

"I know you hit your head, but this is my house."

When he began to shake his head, it amplified the pain. He stopped. "Right now, this is a crime scene." He gestured toward the front door. "Let's go."

Belle's lips formed an O.

After they were out in the snowy driveway, there were footsteps, and then Deputy Paula Stark said, "Boss, you're bleeding."

"I'm fine," he said.

"No, you're not." Belle grasped his arm and drew him toward the pickup. "What happened to you?"

As she opened the door and pushed him down on the passenger seat, he said, "The suspect threw something at me. I didn't duck in time. It felt like a concrete block."

Belle was quiet for a moment. "Perhaps a book?"

"If it was, it was a big book."

"I have a copy of *War and Peace* in the living room."

He went slack-jawed. He never would have guessed she would read something like that. He quickly regained his composure. "You've read *War and Peace*?"

"Not a chance. It's not my genre. It was my father's, and I thought it would make a good decoration."

He turned to Deputy Stark. "Start collecting evidence. I'll go see if there are some footprints in the snow that we can cast." When he went to stand, Belle's hand pressed down on his shoulder. He frowned up at her. "What are you doing?"

"You aren't going anywhere." Belle's voice brooked no argument. "You're injured."

He let out a frustrated groan. He had been so close to catching the suspect, and still the guy got away. Parker was angry with himself. He should have caught them by now.

"Hey, Parker. You okay?" He glanced up to find his brother Michael stepping up to him with a worried look on his face. Michael's newly adopted puppy, Tank, was standing quietly by his side.

"I'm fine." A note of exasperation came through in his voice.

"You don't look fine."

Belle turned to his brother. "Make sure he doesn't move. I'll be right back."

"You can't go in there," Parker said.

"But I have to. You need something for that cut."

"You can't go in there," he said sternly. "It's a crime scene."

She turned to him and pressed her hands to her hips. She pursed her lips as though she were getting ready to launch into him, but it didn't matter what she said, he wasn't going to let her in the house until it was fully processed.

Then she stomped off. He watched her unlock her car. She leaned down and appeared to open the glove box. When she returned, she had a fist full of napkins.

She looked at him. "These are far from sanitary, but you can't just sit there with blood dripping down your face."

He grabbed the napkins and pressed them to the wound. He grimaced at the pain, but he wasn't going to let it stop him. He just needed a bandage, and he'd be fine.

The sound of approaching footsteps had Parker glancing down the driveway. Parker inwardly groaned when he saw his other brothers Colin and Justin headed in his direction.

"Parker, what happened to you?" Colin walked over to him and knelt down next to him. He removed the napkins that were quickly becoming soaked with blood.

"What are you doing?" Parker didn't like his younger brothers fussing over him.

"Here." Belle handed Colin some fresh napkins. "This is all I have *because* Parker won't let me back in the house."

Colin immediately grabbed the napkins. He dabbed at the wound.

"Ow..." Parker jerked away from him.

Colin frowned. "I forgot what a wimp you can be."

Parker glared at him. Now was not the time for one of their juvenile spats, especially when his deputies were close by, and Belle was looking on.

Parker swallowed hard and attempted to keep the frustration out of his voice. "Maybe you should get a gentler touch. Just put a bandage on it. I have work to do."

Colin shook his head. "A bandage isn't going to be enough. You need stitches, some ice, and to be checked for a concussion."

Parker's jaw clenched. He didn't have time for this. The suspect evaded him this time, but next time would be different. He lowered his head and noticed the blood that had dripped onto his coat. He supposed his brother was right.

He lifted his gaze to meet Colin's. "Then just do it."

"Do what?"

"Put in the stitches."

Colin shook his head as he held up his palms. "Oh, no. I'm not doing that."

"Come on." Parker really needed to have his head taken care of so he could get back to work.

"No." Colin's voice was firm as he straightened. "I'm an animal doctor, not a human one."

Belle spoke up. "And it's your face. You want a specialist to do the stitches so there's minimal scarring." She glanced over at Colin. "Sorry. I don't mean that you aren't a great vet—especially since you're Odie's vet." The mention of her missing dog immediately brought a frown to her lips.

Colin nodded. "You're right." He turned his attention to Parker. "I just have one question: what hit you?"

"A book."

Justin arched a brow. "That must be some book."

"It is huge," Belle said. "It's a copy of *War and Peace*."

Justin let out a whistle. "You're lucky your head is still attached."

"Tell me about it," Parker muttered.

"Wait till Mom hears about this." Michael reached for his phone.

Parker frowned. "Don't call her."

"I have to. I promised I would after I checked on you. Of course, I don't have to call, and then she can drive over here to see you for herself."

Parker hesitated. "Fine. Call her."

Just then Parker's phone buzzed. He pulled it from his pocket to find it was Deputy Williams. Parker pressed the phone to his ear. "What did you find?"

"There's an abandoned ATV just off of Dancer Lane. The engine is still warm."

This was the break he'd been waiting for. Parker took the napkins from his brother. He dabbed at his head and then lowered his arm. He went to get to his feet, but Belle reached out and pushed him back into the seat. He frowned at her. At the same time, he felt a cool trickle make its way down the side of his face.

Belle lifted his arm and pressed his hand with the napkins back against his temple. "We need to get to the hospital."

He ignored her. "Williams, secure the ATV. Call Daryl's Garage. Have them haul it back to the shed."

"Yes, sir. I'm on it." Deputy Williams sounded excited to be on the case.

Daryl's ChainUp and Go was the only tow service in town. They had a contract with the sheriff's office. And honestly, they hadn't needed anything towed since Williams got his SUV stuck in the ditch last winter.

When Parker wrapped up his phone conversation, Belle said, "Now we're off to the hospital." When he went to disagree, she held up her hand. "Don't even think of arguing."

His eyes momentarily widened. She'd done a good impression of his mother. It was very impressive or scary. He wasn't quite sure which.

He didn't know how he was supposed to do his job from the hospital. But by then, Belle was flanked by all three of his brothers. Parker expelled a sigh.

"Hey," Michael said, "you have to do this if you're going to charge him with assault."

Parker had never thought of himself as a victim. He had always been on the other side of the badge. He didn't like being a victim. Then again, he was quite certain no one wanted to wear the title either.

In the past, he'd been the one convincing victims to go to the hospital to be checked out. Now here he was fighting the thought of going to the ER.

It wasn't the smell of antiseptic or the needles that had him fighting the trip to the hospital. It was the fact that he would have to acknowledge to himself that the suspect got the best of him.

It was a blow to his pride. He wouldn't make the mistake of underestimating this criminal again.

"Fine. Let's go."

Chapter Eleven

It was unnerving.

And that was putting it mildly.

Belle couldn't believe that someone had broken into her house, not just once but twice. Who does that? At least now she knew why they wanted her at the Christmas party. They wanted her out of the house so they could what? Search it? But for what?

Even though she'd been at the hospital for a few hours while they checked out Parker, she still felt rattled. The good news was they released Parker, but she wasn't sure if that was due to his condition or the fact that he told them point blank that he wasn't staying. And nothing she said would sway him to stay a little longer.

And so it was after midnight when she drove him back to her place. From what Belle could gather from overhearing Parker's phone conversations, the deputies were still there, processing the scene. It sounded like this break-in had been a lot more aggressive. To her, that meant there would be more damage. She dreaded seeing her home damaged.

Every time this person broke into her home, she felt as though she'd been exposed. They'd barged right into her living room, her bedroom, and nosed through her personal things. Just the thought sent a sense of revulsion through her.

In addition, with each home invasion, her sense of security eroded. Would she ever feel safe in her home again? She didn't know.

But the worst was that they took her puppy. They had dangled the hope of getting Odie back to get her out of the house. And in the end, it was all a lie. Who does that?

The one positive thing that had come from this experience was that it brought her and Parker closer together. She honestly didn't think that was possible. He was no longer the sheriff who was lying in wait to pull her over and ticket her.

Instead, he was actually a nice guy who perhaps clung to the rules and laws a little too tightly. But she supposed that everyone had their faults.

Of course, she knew this was all temporary. Come Monday, he'd go back to keeping the streets of Kringle Falls safe. And then she'd be home alone. She wondered if the person who broke in would come back. The thought sent a chill down her spine.

Was it possible that Parker would stay with her until the suspect was caught? Then she realized that wasn't possible. He had to get back to work. He'd already gone out of his way for her.

She paused to give the circumstances of their new relationship some thought. What would you call it? Friends? *No.* That didn't seem quite right. Frenemies? *No.* Because Parker was doing everything he could to help her. She didn't think he was faking his kind gestures and friendliness. So, where did that leave them?

She didn't know. She supposed they were still a work in progress. *Yes.* That sounded right. But where would they end up? As friends? She refused to even consider that they could aspire to something more.

She slowed down and turned into her driveway. There was only one police vehicle in the driveway. She was sure that the other deputy was back patrolling the streets of Kringle Falls. After all, she'd been taking up a lot of their time. Not that it was her fault. There was some horrible criminal who was trying to ruin her life.

Belle pulled the car to a stop and turned off the engine. She turned to Parker. "You heard what the doctor said. You need to rest. You just had twelve stitches put in your head."

"I'm fine." He opened the car door. "I have work to do."

Before she could say more, he was already in the driveway. She rushed to catch up to him. In her hurry, she slipped. She went down, landing on her backside with an *ompf.*

Parker turned and rushed over to her. He held out his hands to her and pulled her upright. "Are you all right?"

His pull was more than she'd been anticipating. She was propelled toward him. She put out her hands, which landed on his muscled chest. If she were to tilt her chin upward, and he were to look down at her, they would be in the perfect position to share a kiss. The thought sent her heart pitter-pattering.

She wondered what it'd be like to be kissed by him. Would it be quick and sweet? Or would it be slow and passionate?

The direction of her thoughts caused her to promptly lower her arms. "Sorry about that."

He looked down at her dress shoes. "Maybe some boots would be better."

Oh sure. Snow boots would have looked awesome with her outfit for the Christmas party. She resisted rolling her eyes. Instead of arguing with him, she turned and headed toward the house. It looked like all of the lights were on both upstairs and downstairs.

Surely, they had to be done collecting evidence by then. Right? All she wanted to do was go to bed and forget about the way this evening had ended. Instead of things getting better, they only seemed to get worse. Now Parker was injured. What else could go wrong?

They entered the house and closed the door when his phone rang. She paused and looked at him, hoping there was a big break in the case. He glanced at the screen and then called upstairs. "Deputy Stark, we're back."

Immediately, his phone stopped ringing, and there were footsteps on the stairs. Paula's eyes widened when she saw Parker. "Boss, you're gonna have a shiner."

He nodded as he pressed his hands to his sides. "Why did you just call me?"

Paula blinked, as though she were gathering her thoughts. "We have full prints this time. Just a couple but they're really good."

"Nice work. Have Williams run them, and hopefully, we'll get a hit."

"Already working on it. So far nothing has popped."

He jutted out his chin. "You almost done here?"

Paula nodded. "Uh. Yeah. I just have to finish the bedroom. It's taken me some time to do the whole house on my own."

Belle couldn't imagine what that must entail. It'd been hours since they left the party, and Paula had been working the house for most of that time.

At this point, Belle felt as though she were going to drop from exhaustion. And then she recalled the doctor saying that Parker had a concussion. Thoughts of curling up in her comfy bed fled from her mind. Her gaze strayed to the over-stuffed armchair in the living room. It looked like that was where she'd be spending her night or what was left of it.

But as she turned, she caught sight of the Christmas tree tipped over. She gasped. The ornaments that had been handed down to her were scattered across the floor. Most of them were shattered.

Tears burned the back of her eyes. How could this have happened? And then she recalled the intruder throwing a book from the nearby end table. He must have knocked the tree over before busting out the window, which was now covered by plywood to block out the cold air.

Paula retreated upstairs. The next thing she knew, she felt Parker come up behind her. His hands came to rest on her shoulders.

"I'm so sorry." His words were soft, but they burrowed deep into her heart.

She wanted to say something to him, but it was taking everything she could do to hold her emotions in. She knew some old ornaments shouldn't mean that much to her, but after losing her family, they felt like her last tangible link to her past.

It was her fault. She shouldn't have put them on the tree. But her mother firmly believed that they didn't belong in a box. They were to be put out and enjoyed.

Parker prompted her to turn around. When his gaze met hers, she saw sympathy in his brown eyes. He pulled her to him. She didn't fight him. The warmth of his hug was like a balm on her broken heart. She reached out and wrapped her arms around him. Her head rested against his chest. She didn't know why she did it. It just felt right in the moment.

She didn't know how long they stood there like that. Her gaze kept taking in the sight. She eagerly sought out any ornaments that could be salvaged. There weren't many, mostly the ones that were still on the tree. Any that landed on the floor were broken, and some were smashed to the point of being unrecognizable.

Once she gathered her emotions, she reluctantly pulled away from his embrace. She looked down at the mess. The next thing she knew, she was kneeling down. She started to pick up the pieces of her past—of her heritage. When Parker brought her a box to put the broken pieces in, she knew they'd eventually make it to the garbage, but this was better than a trash bag.

As she worked, a drop landed on the back of her hand. She raised her hand and felt her cheeks, which were damp with tears. She swiped them away. She wouldn't fall apart again.

The next thing she knew Parker knelt down next to her. He sat back on his heels. "Would it be okay if I helped you?"

His words touched her. No man had ever been so kind to her. Emotions clogged her throat.

In a soft voice, he said, "Belle?"

She couldn't look at him. He would see that she was on the verge of breaking down again. Instead, she nodded and put the box between them.

She didn't know how long they worked quietly together. Paula finished up her work somewhere along the way. Parker excused himself and walked the deputy outside. Belle assumed he wanted to talk more about the case, but he didn't want Belle to overhear. And to be honest, she couldn't deal with any more that evening. After all, it was now the middle of the night. She should go to sleep, but she couldn't, not until she took care of the ornaments.

Parker wasn't gone long. When he stepped up next to her, she thought he would insist that she call it a night, but he didn't. Instead, he quietly settled on the floor next to her and piece by piece they placed the broken ornaments in the box.

For the first time, she noticed how his presence was a comfort to her. The realization shocked her to the point that she gasped.

"What's wrong?" Parker turned to her. "Did you cut yourself?"

She shook her head as she held up her hand, as though to check for a cut. "I'm okay."

She got back to work. As angry as she was with the person who had broken into her home, she blamed herself more. She should have taken the ornaments off the tree after the first break-in. She should have foreseen an accident like this. This whole mess was her fault.

"I should have known better," she muttered to herself.

"What?"

"Nothing."

He was quiet for a moment. "Are you blaming yourself?"

"Yes." The word popped out of her mouth before she could stop it. But it felt good to admit it. And so she kept going. "I should have known better than to put those ornaments on the tree."

"Whoa. Slow down." He sat back on his heels. "What is the point of having something special—something beautiful—if you never get to see it because it's always in a box?"

"You sound like my mother." Her voice cracked with emotion. "But if they had been in a box, they wouldn't be ruined."

He reached over and gave her a one-arm hug. "This isn't your fault. It's the suspect's. And I promise you that we're going to find him, and he is going to pay for what he's done."

They finished picking up as much as they could. Parker got to his feet with the box in his hands. "What would you like me to do with this?"

She shrugged. "It's not like I can repair any of it." She couldn't bring herself to tell him to put the box in the garbage. Instead she said, "Just make it go away."

He solemnly nodded his head.

While he took care of the box, she straightened the tree. She took the remaining ornaments off the tree. She was sad that so few had survived. She carefully took them and placed them on the kitchen island. She proceeded to wrap them in paper towels before placing them in a large rectangular plastic box with a lid.

In the meantime, Parker inquired about the vacuum. She told him it was in the hall closet. She was surprised when he set to work vacuuming the floor. She thought he'd want to go to sleep. He probably did, but he wasn't going to leave her to do this on her own.

She stepped into the living room. When he saw her, he turned off the vacuum. Before he could say anything, she said, "You need to rest."

"I'm not resting until you do."

She opened her mouth to tell him she still had the upstairs to clean up, but she wordlessly pressed her lips together. He was injured and needed to rest. That was more important than the fact that she didn't think she'd be able to sleep that night. All the events of the evening were still rolling around in her mind.

"Fine," she said. "We're done for tonight." Her gaze met his. "Thank you for..." She recalled the image of him kneeling beside her and picking up broken pieces of ornaments, but she couldn't vocalize her feelings in that moment. "For everything."

He stepped closer to her. "Are you going to be all right? I know how much those heirlooms meant to you."

She nodded, not trusting her voice. She moved to the stairs and rushed up them, needing a moment by herself to gather her feelings. When she reached the landing, she came to a sudden halt. A gasp tore from her lungs.

"Belle?" Hurried footsteps sounded. Parker stopped right behind her. "What's..."

He grew quiet as he took in the sight with her. Her belongings were thrown across the hallway in a haphazard fashion. There were random holes in the wall as though someone had been in a rage and punched it. The pictures on the wall were smashed. Broken glass was scattered all over the floor.

This on top of the destroyed ornaments made her stomach take a nauseous lurch. She pressed a hand to her mid-section as tears rushed to her eyes. She blinked repeatedly. Why was this happening to her?

She took a step forward. The crunch of broken glass sounded under her shoe.

"Stop." Parker reached out for her arm.

"No." She pushed his arm away.

Cold dread inched down her spine and consumed her as she stepped toward her bedroom. The closer she got to the doorway, the worse the mess. Dread settled in the pit of her stomach. She couldn't tear her gaze away from the destruction of her home.

It wasn't just glass on the floor; there were clothes, books, and all sorts of things scattered over the floor. When she reached her bedroom doorway, she once more came to a stop. Her blood ran cold as her stomach took another nauseous lurch.

It looked like a tornado had blown through the room. Her bed was literally torn apart. The mattress was thrown against one wall while the box spring was against another wall. The quilt her mother had made her was twisted and tangled around the headboard. Tears rushed to her eyes as her throat tightened, holding back the rush of emotions.

She didn't understand. Why was this happening? What did she do to this person for them to invade her home, take her dog, and destroy her sense of security?

Parker stepped up behind her. His arms wrapped around her chest and gently pulled her back until her head was resting against his broad chest. The heat of his body radiated to her, warming her.

"Wh-Why?" Her mind struggled to make sense of the mess before her. Then again, she wasn't sure any of this was ever going to make sense.

"I don't know." His voice was soft and caring as he tightened his arms around her. "I will catch them. They left a lot of evidence behind this time."

She closed her eyes, blocking out the damage. Her heart ached. Where was Odie? Would she ever see him again?

"Belle, I know it doesn't seem like it now, but everything is going to work out." There was a certainty to his voice.

She wanted to believe him, but when she opened her eyes, she was faced with the harsh reality. "You don't know that."

"I've never been so determined to solve a case in my life."

She turned in his arms so she could look into his eyes. "Who does something like this?" Her voice cracked with emotion. "Why me? Why my puppy?"

"I don't know." Compassion shone in his eyes. "I..." His gaze lowered to her lips and lingered. "I don't know."

She accepted that. Neither one of them had the answers...at least not yet. But she believed they would catch the dognapper and get Odie back.

Her gaze took in the lines on Parker's face and his bloodshot eyes. He was tired. And then there were the stitches and his black eye.

Of their own volition, her fingers reached up to his injured eye. She made sure not to touch the bruised skin. Her fingertips grazed his jaw.

Her gaze returned to his. "How bad does it hurt?"

"It's fine."

Fine wasn't an answer. She felt guilty. "I'm sorry I got you involved in this."

"You don't have to be sorry. You didn't do anything wrong."

"But if it wasn't for me, you wouldn't have been injured."

He shrugged. "It's just part of the job. I'll be fine."

Her fingertips continued to trace the side of his chiseled face. It was as if she couldn't help herself. She was drawn to him in a way that she'd never been attracted to anyone else. When her fingers neared his lips, she was tempted to trace them too.

He sucked in a deep breath. In the next breath, he broke their connected gaze. He released her and took a step back. He felt something growing between them. She could see it in his eyes.

He glanced down as he cleared his throat. "We should go back downstairs. We can sleep at my place."

"No." The answer was quick and firm. When he sent her a questioning look, she said, "This jerk has taken my dog. He's destroyed my family heirlooms. He... I don't know what he was doing in my bedroom. I'm not letting him run me out of my own home."

Parker hesitated. "I understand."

She led the way back downstairs. She had some fresh clothes in the laundry room. After she changed into an old, comfy T-shirt and a pair of sweatpants, she joined Parker in the living room.

He finished fixing up the couch with a blanket and pillow. He turned to her. "Here you go."

She was touched by his gesture. "Thank you. But you take the couch."

He arched a brow. "Where are you planning to sleep?"

She pointed to the navy-blue oversized armchair with a matching ottoman. It was her cozy spot where she liked to get lost in the pages of a good romance. "It's my favorite spot."

"But it's a chair."

"A very comfortable chair." She always kept a red and white log cabin quilt hung over the back of the chair.

His gaze searched hers. She stared directly back at him. Her gaze was unwavering as she crossed her arms.

He sighed. "You aren't going to change your mind, are you?"

She shook her head. "You're the one with your head stitched together. Not me."

"Fine. But I'm doing this under protest."

With only the soft glow from the light above the kitchen sink, they both settled in for what was left of the wintry night. Belle found herself grateful for the quilt because once she sat down, she noticed the cold seeping into her bones. If she remembered correctly the forecast said the temperature was supposed to dip down into the single digits. *Ugh.* And this was only the beginning of winter.

She was determined to stay awake and watch over Parker, since he had a concussion. Yet, the darkness called to her, and her eyelids grew heavy. At one point, they drifted shut. A few moments later, she opened them. She yawned. This was going to be the longest night of her life.

She listened to his deep, even breaths. At least one of them was getting some rest. She knew if she just sat there in the dark doing nothing, she would be fast asleep in no time.

She reached for her phone. She curled up in the chair and pulled up a book on her phone. It didn't take her long to get lost in the words. The only problem was that her eyelids were so heavy, and she was having a problem staying focused on the words. And every minute or two a yawn would plague her.

Still, she persisted. She wouldn't fall asleep. She yawned again. The words on her phone blurred. She blinked, and they came back into focus. And then she began to read again.

Chapter Twelve

His head hurt.

His neck had a crick in it. And his back ached from the lumpy couch. Even so, he wouldn't be anywhere else.

The following morning, Parker glanced over at Belle. She was curled up beneath the red and white quilt. She had a peaceful look on her face. He was grateful she was able to rest and not have nightmares about the break-ins.

She must have been exhausted, because she didn't move when he got up. He grabbed a shower and put on fresh clothes from the duffel bag he'd grabbed at his place. When he came downstairs, Belle was still asleep, but she appeared to have a frown on her face. He thought of rousing her but decided that her sleep took priority.

He grabbed his coat and cell phone. Out on the back porch, he rang the sheriff's office. The conversation was brief. The ATV was reported stolen a couple of days ago from a nearby town. His deputy talked to the owner, but they didn't have a clue who had taken it.

The prints matched the prior ones. It would appear there was only one suspect. As before, the prints didn't get any hits in AFIS (Automated Fingerprint Identification System).

Most career criminals would have been in and out without wasting their time tearing the house apart. A professional would know the longer they were in the house, the greater the chance they'd be caught. This person was a novice, which meant they'd make more mistakes. That was how they were going to catch them.

His people had also checked with local ERs and veterinarian offices to see if anyone showed up in need of stitches in their hands or arms. So far, they didn't have a lead.

He stepped back inside the cozy warm kitchen. After ditching his coat and boots, he washed up. Then he glanced in the fridge. When he closed the door, he noticed the colorful invitation to the Kringle's party. This must be how the suspect knew Belle had planned to attend. That answered one of his many questions.

He continued searching through the cabinets. He was trying to come up with an idea of what to make for breakfast. When he saw the syrup, he knew what to make...pancakes. Everybody liked those, right?

With the flour, sugar, vanilla, eggs, butter, and milk on the counter, he set to work. But with it being the holiday season, he felt as though he should do a little extra. He wanted to bring back a little holiday spirit for Belle.

A little bit later, he had a stack of pancakes. Feeling pleased with himself for not burning any of them, he walked back into the living room.

He really didn't want to disturb her, but he had to leave to head to the office. There were reports he needed to review. He didn't want to leave her alone, but he also wanted to catch the person who had been tormenting her.

He knelt down beside her. He couldn't resist moving a long lock of her silky auburn hair from her face. "Belle?"

She didn't respond.

He tried again. "Belle, breakfast is ready."

Her eyes fluttered open. At first, she looked at him with a blank stare. It made him think of his mother's old saying: the lights are on, but no one's home. It definitely described Belle in that moment.

She blinked a couple of times and yawned. It was then that he realized he'd forgotten something.

"I'll be right back." He straightened and went into the kitchen. He grabbed a mug and filled it with some fresh-brewed coffee. He added some creamer and sweetener, just like he'd seen her do. Then he returned to the living room to find that Belle hadn't moved.

He held the cup out to her. "You might want this."

A smile lifted her rosy lips. "Thank you."

When she reached out to take the mug, their fingers touched. It was as though static electricity entered his fingertips and worked its way up his arm. The sensation settled in his chest and set his heart pounding.

His gaze met and held hers. She was so beautiful and not just on the outside. Any man would be lucky to have a woman like her in their life, but that man wasn't him. They'd always been opposites. And that hadn't changed over the years.

He knew all about opposites. His last relationship had ended because his fiancée said he was too stuck in his ways. She needed someone who wanted some adventure in his life.

Parker got enough adventure just doing his job. From dealing with wildlife that ended up in wrong places to pulling over a car for a moving violation. He always wondered what sort of person he was going to face. Overwhelmingly, the people were reasonable, but you just never knew.

His gaze moved to where his fingertips were still touching hers. It felt like time had stood still, and yet it had only been a mere couple of seconds. His heart was still hammering in his chest. He pulled his hand back, breaking the connection.

Without a word, he straightened. He strode into the kitchen, where he at last was able to take a deep breath. What was wrong with him? He was acting like he was back in high school when he'd had the biggest crush on her. But that was ages ago.

He moved to the fridge and grabbed the butter. He placed it on the table along with the syrup. While he stayed busy, he forced his thoughts to the case—the whole reason they were near inseparable. If he could solve this case, he could go back to his solitary life and forget about the way she felt in his arms or how he could so easily lose himself in those mesmerizing blue eyes of hers.

Just then he heard the shuffling of feet. He glanced up to find a sleepy Belle headed toward him. She looked so adorable with a rosy hue in her cheeks and her hair mussed up. She looked much more relatable than her usual polished appearance.

When she took a seat at the table, he asked, "Would you like some pancakes?"

Her eyes widened. "You made pancakes?" When he nodded, she asked, "But how? I'm out of pancake mix."

He grinned. "I made it from scratch."

She shrugged. "I never knew a guy who was such a good cook."

"Then you've been hanging out with the wrong guys." And in that moment, he knew he meant it. He wanted her to continue to hang out with him, but how long would that work before she made an exit like his ex?

She turned the plate around and gaped when she looked at the pancake. "You made a Santa hat pancake?" She continued to stare at it. "You even made his hat red."

"Uh-huh. Thought you needed some holiday cheer. I would have put whipped cream on the tassel and the rim, but you didn't have any. Maybe next time." He couldn't believe he'd added that last part. It wasn't like he was going to have an opportunity to make her pancakes again.

He remembered how much it had hurt when Lori dumped him. Of course, if he'd paid attention to his relationship, he would have seen the signs. But they'd been together almost two years by then, and he'd let himself get comfortable in the relationship—obviously too comfortable. He'd just taken it for granted that they'd get married and grow old together. He'd never been more wrong.

It took him a couple of tries to find the correct cabinet to retrieve a plate. And then he served himself a pancake. He sat down beside her at the table.

After taking her first bite, he noticed she didn't eat anymore. He tasted his pancake to make sure he hadn't mixed up the sugar and salt. *Nope.* It wasn't that. Then again, maybe she just didn't like pancakes.

"Can I make you something else?" he asked.

She looked at him with a blank expression on her face, as though she had been lost in her thoughts and hadn't heard him.

He tried again. "Do you want something else to eat? Just name it, and I'll get it for you."

Her eyes widened, as though she were surprised by the offer. "What if I want a breakfast burrito?"

"Do you?"

She shook her head. "The point is that you can't offer to make me anything. I don't have a lot of ingredients. In fact, I need to go shopping, so I'm set for the week."

"Well, if you want a burrito or whatever, I'll just drive into town and get it for you."

Her brows rose. "You'd really do that?"

"I would."

The smile returned to her lips. "Well, thank you. But the pancakes are good."

"Then why aren't you eating?"

She hesitated, as though trying to decide how honest to be with him. "I'm just trying to wrap my mind around putting my house back together and..."

"And what?"

She sighed. "Trying to figure out who keeps breaking in and what they want. Other than the sentimentality, the stuff in here isn't worth much."

"What about an antique?"

She gave it some thought. "The only thing I can think of is my grandmother's china."

"Is it rare or anything?"

"Not that I know of. I would think if it was that, my grandmother or mother would have mentioned it. There's no way those dishes are valuable enough to have a criminal commit repeated break-ins." She shook her head. "I just don't believe it."

"I understand. But there is something in this house." He paused to give it some thought. "How long has your family owned this house?"

"My grandfather built it. It's always been in the family."

He gave it some more thought. Whatever the criminal wanted was here and either Belle was unaware of its presence or she overlooked it. But how did he jar her thoughts?

"Maybe it's a piece of jewelry."

She immediately shook her head. "I don't have anything valuable."

"How about a diamond ring?" The breath hitched in his throat as he waited for her response.

Sure, they'd grown up in the same small town, but he didn't listen to all of the gossip. And he didn't keep up with the goings on with Belle's love life. For all he knew she could have been engaged five times.

"No. I don't have any diamond rings."

He released the pent-up breath. He didn't know why it should matter to him whether she'd been engaged in the past. After all, it hadn't even been a year since the plug was pulled on his own engagement. And now that it was over, he was able to look back with clear eyes and see that they were never meant to be together—not for the long haul.

"Let's go see what's in your jewelry box," he said. "Maybe there's something you forgot about." When she frowned at him, he said, "I'm serious. You might have forgotten a gift you were given or an heirloom."

She shook her head. "It's not that. It's the fact that I don't know where my jewelry box is. My bedroom looks like a tornado blew through it."

She was right. He was so focused on solving this case that he'd forgotten they had a lot of work to do that day. He thought about his desire to go into the office, but he supposed he could just have his staff email him the necessary reports.

He picked up his fork. "Well, then eat up. You're going to need your energy if we're going to clean up this house."

Her brows drew together. "You're going to help?"

"Of course. Friends help friends." It wasn't until he uttered the words that he wondered if he'd overstepped. His gaze searched hers.

Her blue eyes sent him a questioning look. "You think of us as friends?"

He shrugged. "I never thought of us as enemies." It didn't exactly answer her question. He didn't know why labeling their relationship made him feel so uncomfortable. When she arched a brow at him, he said, "It's true."

"And I suppose all of those tickets you wrote me was just your way of saying hi."

"Hey, those tickets were all legit. It's not my fault you think the speed limit is just a suggestion."

"That's not true!"

This time he was the one to arch a brow at her. "Maybe you were speeding because you wanted me to pull you over."

Her mouth formed a big O. Once she regained her composure, there was color in her cheeks when she said, "And why would I want you to do that?"

"Because you just can't stay away from me." He sent her a teasing grin.

"Oh, boy." She rolled her eyes. "You need to work on your pick-up lines."

"That wasn't a pick-up line." Was it?

Was he interested in Belle? *No.* The answer was swift, perhaps too swift. But he wasn't going to let himself get distracted. He was there to do a job. Nothing more.

Chapter Thirteen

I T WAS AWFUL.

But thankfully, she didn't have to face it alone.

Belle stood at the doorway of her bedroom, which looked like a disaster zone. Cleaning wasn't exactly her thing. She did it when she had to. She was far from a slob but nowhere close to being tidy. She was somewhere in between.

She'd thanked Parker for offering to help her clean, but she told him it wasn't necessary. He insisted on staying and helping her with the house. But before they could get started, there was a knock at the door. She wasn't expecting anyone.

She turned to Parker. "Someone for you?"

He shook his head. "I'm not expecting anyone." When she started downstairs, he said, "Maybe I should get it."

She stopped and glanced back at him. "I'm not going to live in fear."

This criminal had already stolen enough from her. She wasn't going to give up her sense of independence. She arched a brow at Parker. He hesitated for a moment. She appreciated that he wanted to keep her safe, but she wasn't going to back down on this. At last, he sighed and nodded for her to keep going.

She turned and continued downstairs. When she swung the door open, her mouth momentarily gaped. It was Parker's parents. Because they all lived in a small town and having grown up with Parker, Belle knew his parents. They would share the occasional greeting in town, but they'd never been to each other's homes. This was a first.

"Hi." Belle plastered a smile on her face. "You must be here to see Parker. Come on in out of the cold."

Belle stepped back and pulled the door wide open. When his parents stepped inside, a gust of wintry air followed them in. As she closed the door, she realized she should have started the fireplace, but she'd been so distracted with the daunting task of cleaning up the upstairs that she hadn't thought about trudging out in the cold to retrieve wood from the firewood shed.

As if on cue, Parker stepped up behind her. "Mom. Dad. What are you doing here? Is something wrong?"

His mother sent her son a reassuring smile. "Everything is okay with us." Her gaze moved to Belle. "It's you that we're worried about. Michael was just filling us in on what all went on last night." His mother's gaze moved to her son. "Are you all right?"

While Parker assured his parents that he was fine, Belle immediately felt guilty. Parker's injury was all her fault. *Okay. Maybe it isn't entirely my fault.* After all, she wasn't the one who had struck him. Still, it was her home and her book that struck him.

"So, what are you doing here?" Parker asked once more.

His mother, Tricia, smiled as she slipped off her coat. "We're here to help." She gently elbowed his father, John. "Aren't we?"

"Uh, yes." He smiled. "Yes, we are. I hear there's a window that needs to be replaced. I picked up some glass on the way over."

"That's great," Parker said.

At least one of them was happy about this turn of events. This was not the way she wanted to get to know Parker's parents better. Not that there was any reason for her to get to know his parents better. As the ramifications of what she was thinking sank in, she inwardly groaned. Ever since Parker had become her bodyguard, she hadn't been thinking clearly.

"Well, I'll let you visit." Belle was anxious to put some distance between her and Parker. "I have some cleaning to do upstairs."

Tricia's brows creased as worry clouded her eyes. "Was that horrid person up there too?"

This question made Belle wonder how much his parents really knew. Belle nodded. "I don't know what they were searching for, but they destroyed a lot of stuff." Thoughts of the broken ornaments poked at her heart. "At least now they should realize that whatever they're searching for, isn't here. I just need them to give Odie back."

"Your poor little puppy must be missing you something fierce." Sympathy oozed from Tricia's voice. She turned to Parker. "Are you close to catching him?"

Belle noticed the brief frown that flashed over Parker's face. "Mom, you know I can't discuss ongoing cases with you."

"But Belle needs this to be over and her puppy returned to her."

Belle could see the fine lines deepen on his face. She'd seen that look before when he was getting frustrated with her.

When he spoke, it was in an even tone. "I understand. And we're doing everything we can."

Tricia arched a brow as she looked at him. "Then why are you still here?"

"It's my day off." As though sensing that answer wasn't what his mother wanted to hear, he said, "And I have a window to replace. We're not sure what the suspect is searching for and when or if he'll return, but I want the house secure."

"Your father can help you. We have to hurry," Tricia said. "Tonight is caroling."

Parker vocally groaned as he rolled his eyes.

"Oh, don't be that way." His mother lightly slapped him on the arm. "It's tradition." She looked at Belle. "You sing, don't you?"

"In the car with the radio turned up." Belle smiled.

"Good enough. Now, everyone get back to work."

Work? Belle's mouth opened, but no words came out. What exactly did his mother mean? Was she planning to help the guys with the window? That must be it.

"Okay," Belle said. "Just yell if you need me."

As she started up the steps, she sensed Tricia was right behind her. It would be a little awkward to stop on the steps and ask her where she was going, so Belle continued up to the landing.

There was hardly any place to stand that wasn't covered by a mess of broken glass from wall hangings, overturned wooden shelving units, knick knacks, or any number of other items.

"Oh, my goodness." Tricia's eyes widened as she took in the sight. "I'm so sorry."

"It isn't the items that I care about that much." Belle's thoughts quickly turned to the broken heirloom ornaments. They were the exception. "But I don't understand why they took Odie."

Tricia reached over and placed her hand on Belle's arm. "I don't think any of us understand what gets into people's minds sometimes." She glanced down at the mess. "Let's get this cleaned up. You can't even walk around up here. I'll have the guys bring up some supplies."

Without another word to Belle, his mother called out to the guys and told them exactly what they were going to need, starting with a broom and dust pan. Once they could walk around, they sorted things into three piles: keep as is, fix it, and straight to the trash.

More ended up in the trash than she'd expected. It was like the person who broke in went into a total rage when they couldn't find what they were searching for. Some of the stuff that was broken appeared to have nothing to do with whatever he wanted. Like the framed pictures on the wall. Why break them?

As they cleaned, his mother talked about nothing in particular. Belle knew his mother was trying to put her at ease, but it wasn't working. Belle's emotions felt like they were on a roller coaster ride.

She was embarrassed to have Tricia going through her personal belongings, not that there was anything to be embarrassed about. It was just an awkward situation. Although, she'd much rather have Parker's mother help than have Parker picking up her underwear. Just the thought set her cheeks ablaze.

When she went to put them away, she found one of her dresser drawers was broken. Tricia insisted that her husband could fix it. Whoever had broken it was a very angry person. There was no other explanation for the degree of damage done. She didn't even want to think about what the person was doing to Odie. Every time she let herself think about the sweetest dog in the world, tears rushed to her eyes.

While they worked upstairs, Parker, his dad, and his brother Colin, who showed up a little bit ago, replaced her window in the living room—the one the burglar had broken the night before.

For lunch, Parker's father ran out and picked up submarine sandwiches for everyone. Belle was truly touched that the Bishop family was pitching in and helping to clean up her house. It was so sweet of them. Now she knew why under his grumpy sheriff persona, Parker was actually a sweet guy.

When she finished making her bed, Belle turned to Tricia. "Thank you so much for helping. I don't know how to thank you."

There was a twinkle in Tricia's eyes. "You can thank me by coming over this evening for some beef vegetable soup and then go caroling. We always need more people."

The first part of the plan sounded good. The second part had her hesitating. "I'm not a good singer."

Tricia waved off her concerns. "You don't have to be."

"I don't?" She was confused. Wasn't the point of caroling to sing to people?

Tricia shook her head. "I'll tell you a secret. My husband can't sing, so he lip-syncs."

"Really?" After her surprised reaction slipped past her lips, Belle clamped them together.

Tricia was unfazed as she nodded. "Not many people know. And he never tells anyone that he's faking it the whole time. But no one has to be a professional singer. It's all for fun. So, you should use your voice, well, if you're comfortable doing it."

"Thanks. I'll think about it." And then a thought came to her. "What about Parker? Does he sing?"

Tricia nodded. "He has a beautiful voice, but he rarely uses it. I can't remember the last time I got him to go caroling. That's why I'm hoping you can get him to go this evening."

"Me?" She pressed a hand to her chest. "I don't think I'm the person to get him to go."

"Sure, you are. If you were to ask him, I'm sure he would do it." Tricia stopped from hanging up one of Belle's blouses and looked directly at her. "My son can be stubborn, and sometimes he can't see what's right in front of his face. Just give him some time. He'll come around."

The heat returned to Belle's cheeks. If she didn't know better, she would think his mother was trying to set them up. But she wouldn't do that, would she?

Tricia hung the top in the closet. "Is there anything else you need done up here?"

Belle shook her head. "Thank you so much. I never would have gotten this done today without your help."

"I'm just sorry that someone broke in here and did all of this damage. They obviously don't have any Christmas spirit in their heart." Tricia moved to the bedroom doorway and paused. "I'll just go get the guys to haul out the trash."

After Parker's mother headed downstairs, Belle took a moment to look around. Her bedroom was back to normal. Then again, a "new normal" would be a better description.

The lamp that had been next to her bed since she was a little girl was now gone—the brass base and hundreds of tiny glass pieces was all that remained. The remnants would be hauled out to the garbage along with numerous other knickknacks, picture frames, and there was even a wooden chair that had been smashed to pieces. The amount of destruction made her sick to her stomach to think about. She had to believe the culprit was going to be caught, and she'd be reunited with Odie. It was her only Christmas wish this year.

She heard the rumble of Parker's voice just outside the bedroom. He was certainly turning out to be different than she'd pictured him all of these years. She was sorry she'd taken so long to get to know him better.

Chapter Fourteen

WHAT WAS SHE DOING?

Parker couldn't believe his mother was blatantly playing matchmaker. She knew he didn't go caroling, and yet she'd gone around him and included Belle. He couldn't let Belle go walking around town without protection.

Even though he didn't know who had broken into her house, he knew the person was becoming unhinged. The level of anger needed to do the damage inside her house was off the charts.

The suspect was taking chances. It wouldn't be out of bounds to think they might try to grab Belle as a way of getting her to reveal the whereabouts of whatever it was they were searching for.

The good news was that they had the suspect's DNA from the blood on the broken glass and his fingerprints. When they caught the person, they would have a solid link between the suspect and the crime. And it didn't hurt that he'd assaulted a law enforcement officer.

Since Parker had a responsibility to keep Belle safe, he was now seated at his mother's dining room table along with Michael, Candi, his parents and Belle. They'd just finished having soup and fresh-baked bread. It'd been a while since he'd had his mother's home-baked bread, so he'd had an extra slice.

"I love all of your decorations," Belle said to his mother.

"Thank you. I've been collecting them for years. Sometimes, I think I have too many. And then I find a new decoration, and I can't resist it."

The family groaned, including him. His mother had a problem with Christmas decorations. There wasn't a room in the house that hadn't been decorated, including both of the bathrooms. His parents' Victorian-style home had electric candles in each of the windows. Even a pine tree in the yard had twinkle lights. And there was a giant snowman in the front yard.

"It's time to go meet the group at Kringle Park for the caroling." His mother beamed.

Everyone stood and filled their hands with dishes to carry to the kitchen. There wasn't much talk as everyone rushed to clean up before they left.

At one point, he leaned over to Belle. "Are you sure you want to do this?"

She turned her head to look at him, and then she whispered. "I take it you don't want to."

What was he supposed to say? That singing was the last thing he wanted to do, but if she was going, then he wanted to be with her. *Wait. That isn't right. Is it?*

Definitely not. He would go because he wanted to keep her safe. Yes, that was it. Still, he couldn't help but ponder his earlier thought. Did he want to be around Belle just because he liked her?

"Parker?" Belle's gaze searched his.

"Uh..." He struggled to recall what they'd been previously talking about, and then he noticed everyone had left them alone in the kitchen. "We should get going before they leave without us."

"Would that be so bad?" Belle walked away.

Had he heard her correctly? Did she want to spend time alone with him? His pulse picked up its pace. Or was he just reading too much into her offhand comment? *Probably.*

As he puzzled over the questions and answers, he joined her by the front door. Everyone but them was bundled up for a chilly walk through town. *Oh, boy.*

Why hadn't she gone caroling before?

Belle totally enjoyed singing Christmas carols. Even though she'd been nervous in the beginning and had initially lip-synced, by ten minutes into it, she was using her voice. No one seemed to care that she wasn't the greatest singer. When she figured this out, she relaxed and just enjoyed the experience.

Of course, she noticed that Parker wasn't enjoying the evening as much as she was. As though he sensed she was staring at him, he turned his head until their gazes met. He sent her a smile, but he didn't even fake singing, "We Wish You A Merry

Christmas." She wasn't going to make an issue of it. She was just glad he was there.

It was surprising to find how quickly she'd gotten used to having him around. Of course, all of that would end tomorrow when they both went back to their jobs. And it was probably for the best, because if they spent any more time together, it might start to seem like they had a real relationship, instead of him being near her to catch a criminal.

Her thoughts turned to Odie. As his image formed in her mind, her heart ached. She was really starting to have doubts if she would ever see him again. And she missed him terribly.

Parker leaned over and whispered in her ear, "Is everything all right?"

Not missing a beat, she said, "Sure. Why?"

"You stopped singing, and you had a sad look on your face."

"I was thinking about Odie. I really wish he was here. Although, he wouldn't enjoy the caroling. He hates the cold. He'd rather be at home curled up with a blanket on the couch."

"I can't honestly blame him."

Just then Parker's mother, who was standing in front of them, turned an arched brow. Belle felt like a kid again. She let out a nervous giggle. Apparently they weren't whispering as quietly as Belle had thought.

She turned her attention back to the carols. They were most of the way through their planned area when her phone began to ring. She was mortified that she hadn't thought to turn off the ringer. She stepped away from the group. Parker followed her.

With warm, fuzzy gloves on, she couldn't just grab it from her coat pocket. And so it kept ringing while she yanked off a glove. Finally, she pulled the phone from her pocket but before she silenced it, she noticed the number on the screen wasn't one she recognized.

Her heart clenched. Was this the dognapper? She froze.

Parker was on his phone, talking to someone. He read off the phone number. And then he placed his hands on her shoulders. "Answer it and put it on speaker."

Her hands were trembling as she pressed the buttons. "Hello."

"If you want to see your dog again, give it to me." The male voice rumbled with anger.

"Please. Give me Odie back." Her voice cracked with emotion. She struggled not to cry in fear for her dog. "He didn't do anything, and he must be so scared."

"You should have thought of it before you hid it from me." His voice was harsh and clipped.

Her heart was pounding so loud it echoed in her ears. "I...I don't know what you're talking about."

There was a distinct pause. "Don't play with me."

"I'm not. Tell me what I need to do to get Odie back."

"Bring the jewelry box to the waterfall tonight at nine and be alone, if you want your dog back. If you aren't alone, the deal is off."

The phone went dead.

Belle turned to Parker. "He hung up. Do... Do you think Odie's okay?"

Parker reached out and drew her to him. He held her for a moment. In his arms, she gathered her emotions. This was about getting Odie home, not the riot of emotions swirling in the pit of her stomach.

When she pulled back, Parker looked directly in her eyes. "What jewelry box?"

Her thoughts were jumbled. Her hands were still trembling. "I don't know what he's talking about."

"Come on." He wrapped an arm around her waist and escorted her to his pickup.

Once they were both inside, and the engine was started, he turned to her. "Do you know what he's talking about?"

"I told you, no. Do you think he still has Odie? I didn't hear him in the background." She worried her bottom lip.

"Odie is fine." Parker's voice was firm and reassuring.

"Then why didn't he say he'd bring him to the meeting spot?" She didn't trust the dognapper, not one little bit. But she would do anything it took to get Odie back.

"I don't know." He put the truck into gear and stepped on the accelerator. "We need to head to your place."

"For what?"

"The jewelry box. Do you think it's the one you have in your bedroom?"

She shook her head. "I've had that since I was a kid and the only value it has is in sentimentality."

"Okay. Do you have another jewelry box?"

She did her best to silence the worried voices in her head. It took a moment, and then it came to her. "I remember. I picked up an old one at an estate sale not long ago. It needs some work, so I put it in the garage. I thought I'd work on it this summer." She couldn't believe that's what all of this trouble was about. "I just can't imagine what he wants with it. It's pretty or it will be when it's sanded and refinished, but it isn't worth any money."

As he drove, he was quiet, as though thinking over what she'd told him. She became lost in her own thoughts as she wondered if she was about to get Odie back. She was willing to do what the dognapper asked of her.

But that wasn't the only thing on her mind that snowy evening. As she watched the snowflakes make their way to the ground, memories came rushing back to her.

"What are you thinking about?" Parker's voice drew her from her thoughts.

As the snow fell, covering the roadway, her thoughts were swept back in time. "I was thinking about a night like this one." She got caught up in the past. "It was my senior year, and I was having a blast. Serena was throwing a party up at her parents' cabin. I heard that you were going to be there. I guess I was driving too fast, and the car went off the road into a ditch."

"Did you get hurt?"

"Not like you're thinking." She paused as she summoned her courage to admit the rest. "I called my parents to come get me." The mantle of guilt slid over her shoulders, weighing her down. "If only I hadn't been so insistent about sneaking off to that party. Of course, my parents didn't know I was going to a party. They thought I was going to Serena's house to study, which just makes me feel worse."

Parker reached over and took her hand into his own. He laced their fingers and gave her hand a squeeze. He didn't say anything. He didn't need to. His touch was reassuring and gave her the strength she needed to finish her story.

"If it wasn't for me lying, they'd still be alive. If they knew it was a party, they never would have let me go." Her heart ached as she peeled back the old scabs.

"I'm positive the accident wasn't your fault. And I don't think your parents would want you blaming yourself for what happened. They loved you. They'd want you to be happy."

"And if I had been honest and kept my word to my parents, the accident wouldn't have happened."

He was quiet for a moment. "I'm sorry that all of this is bringing up bad memories for you."

"Me too."

But she'd made a decision. She was going to keep her word to the dognapper and do exactly what he'd asked of her. She knew how severe the consequences could be when she broke her word. And that sweet, loving puppy was counting on her to get this right. She wouldn't let him down.

They were almost to her house when Parker said, "There has to be something in the jewelry box."

She shook her head. "There isn't. I looked in all of the drawers and stuff."

"I'm telling you there has to be something in it. Nobody goes through what the suspect has done without searching for something important. When we get to the house, I need you to get the jewelry box. We're going to find out what is so important."

"Okay." She just wanted this to be over. She wanted Odie home and this person to go away—far away.

Two minutes later, Parker wheeled into the driveway. The pickup hadn't even come to a full stop, and she already had the door open. She had less than an hour to find the jewelry box and get back into town. Tonight, she was getting Odie back. She refused to accept any other outcome.

She ran to the detached garage. The side door was locked. She reached for her keys, only to realize that she'd left her purse in Parker's truck. With a groan, she turned and ran back to the pickup.

Parker stopped in the driveway. "What's wrong?"

"I forgot my purse." She stomped past him.

After she retrieved her purse, she ran toward the garage. She slipped on some ice and fell on her butt. *Ouch!*

Parker rushed up to her. "Are you okay?"

No. She wasn't okay. Frustration pumped through her. This was important, and she couldn't even stay on her feet. When Parker held a hand out to her, she grabbed it and pulled herself to her feet.

"Thank you." She headed to the side door on the garage.

When she stopped in front of the door, she reached into her purse. Why did she have so much stuff in it? She never really noticed before, but now it was impeding her search for the keys. Blindly, she moved her hand around in her purse. It appeared her keys had sunk to the bottom of her bag.

"What's the matter?" Parker asked.

"Nothing." At the very bottom, her fingers wrapped around her keys. "I've got them."

She pulled the keyring out. Next was sorting through the keys. At last, she had the right one. But when she went to insert it into the lock, she noticed that her hand was trembling. She stabbed at the lock a couple of times and missed each time.

Parker's warm hand closed over hers. "Here, let me give it a try."

There wasn't time to argue. She relinquished the keys. On his first try, he inserted the key and turned. The door opened. He flipped on the lights.

Inside were stacks of cardboard boxes, so much so that she could no longer park her car in the garage.

Parker didn't say anything, but he paused at the doorway like he wasn't sure what to do. Heat warmed her cheeks as she brushed past him. And yet when she was in the garage, she wasn't even sure where exactly she'd put the jewelry box.

When she glanced over her shoulder at Parker, she felt compelled to say something. "After my parents died, uh...my therapist suggested that I make some room for myself in the house. It wasn't easy. In fact, it was one of the hardest things I've ever done."

"I can't imagine."

"Anyway," she rushed on, "I wasn't ready to get rid of the things. Losing them was still too fresh, so I moved the boxes out here. I promised myself that in a few months, I would go through them. But a few months turned into more than ten years, and I still haven't gone through them."

"Maybe you just need some help so that the weight of it all isn't on your shoulders."

Was he offering to help her clean out her garage? It sure sounded like it to her. Her gaze moved over the big boxes that were piled three and four deep. Maybe he was right. With a little help, it could distract her from all of the memories encapsulated in each box.

She tucked away the thought and moved to the boxes. Time was quickly ticking down. She ripped open the first box and peered inside. It had clothes that should be donated. *Another day. Not today.* She closed it. When she went to move it, Parker appeared by her side and took the box for her.

"I put the jewelry box in one of these. I didn't want it to get damaged before I had a chance to work on it. But I can't remember which box."

"We'll find it." There was a note of confidence in his tone.

She hoped he was right because Odie was counting on her not to mess this up.

She continued opening box after box. After she'd worked her way around the garage, she was exasperated. "Why does everything have to be so hard?"

Tears burned the backs of her eyes. Parker reached out and gently pulled her into his arms. Her head came to rest on his broad shoulder.

"I'm sorry you're going through this." His deep voice was soft and comforting. "But it's all going to work out. We're so close to getting Odie back. You just have to keep going."

He was right. She could do this. And hopefully, by the time she went to bed, Odie would be by her side.

She pulled back. Her gaze scanned the garage, and then she spotted some boxes on her father's workbench. She went there. They were too tall on the bench so Parker lowered them to the ground for her.

When she opened the second box, she gasped. At last, she'd found the jewelry box. There wasn't anything fancy about it. It had more classic, subtle lines.

She lifted it. "This is it."

"Great." He reached out for it. "Let's take it in the house and see what we're dealing with."

As they stepped out of the garage, big snowflakes fluttered down, landing on them. Even though she normally loved a wintry evening, this evening she didn't love. Not at all.

She glanced into the darkness and wondered if the dognapper was watching them. Did he see that they'd found the jewelry box? And if so, did that mean he'd bring Odie to the park? He better or he wasn't getting the jewelry box.

In the kitchen, she flicked on the lights. They kicked off their boots by the door. While he placed the jewelry box on the kitchen island, she slipped off her winter coat. She flung it over the back of one of the stools.

She quietly watched as he examined the jewelry box. He opened each drawer and door. There was nothing inside, just like she'd said. Belle sat up straighter when he once again pulled out each drawer. She leaned in close as one by one, he felt around in each opening, searching for a secret compartment. *Please, let there be something there.*

"I don't understand," Belle said. "Why does he want this?"

Parker continued to stare at the jewelry box. "We're missing something."

She checked the time. She only had nineteen minutes to get back to the park and leave the jewelry box. "It doesn't matter. We have the jewelry box. And now I can get Odie back."

Parker nodded as he continued to stare at the box.

"I'm going to change my jeans." When Parker sent her a puzzled look, she added, "They got wet when I fell in the snow."

He once more nodded. "Then we can go."

"We?"

He arched a brow. "You didn't think you were going alone, did you?"

"Yes." She pressed her hands to her hips. "Yes, I did."

He shook his head. "Not going to happen."

"But I have to. Didn't you hear the guy on the phone? He told me to come alone or no deal." Standing no more than a foot from him, she looked into his eyes—dreamy brown eyes. In their depths, she saw his concern. She spoke softly. "You don't have to worry. I'm going to be all right."

"Belle..."

"This is just going to be a quick exchange." She reached out, resting her hand on his shoulder. Her gaze never left his. "It's sweet of you to worry, but this is Kringle Falls where nothing ever happens."

"Well, something has happened now. And we still don't know anything about the suspect."

"As long as I give him what he wants, he'll give me Odie."

Parker shook his head. "It might not be that easy. You have no idea what might happen."

"And you worry too much. I appreciate all of your help, but I have to do this alone."

A muscle in his jaw flexed, as though he were trying to hold back his disagreement. He stared into her eyes, making her already racing heart beat faster. "I can't let you go alone."

"You can't stop me. I have to do whatever is necessary to get Odie back." Knowing that time wasn't on her side, she didn't wait for his response. She turned on her heel and headed for the stairs.

She glanced over her shoulder and noticed him staring at the jewelry box like he was expecting it to reveal its secrets to him. She hoped that was the case, but either way, it was her ticket to getting back her sweet puppy. Tonight, she'd be fussing over Odie and tucking him in for the night. She couldn't wait.

Chapter Fifteen

There had to be something he was missing.

Parker stared at the wooden jewelry box. To him, it was a big jewelry box. The outside was carved with flowers, hearts, and swirls. He didn't see a name of a company, so he wondered if it was handmade. If so, there may well be a hidden compartment.

The top of the box didn't move. It had two wooden doors that had little brass handles. And when he opened them there was a row of little drawers to the left and an open space to the right to hang necklaces. At the bottom of the jewelry box, there was a big drawer.

While Belle was upstairs changing into some dry clothes, he continued to puzzle over the jewelry box. He opened the doors and once more took out each of the little drawers. He studied each of them from top to bottom. He was certain there was nothing special about them. He set them aside.

Then he focused on the rest of the jewelry box. He turned it this way and that way. He knocked on this wall and that wall. And then he noticed that there might be an open space at the top of the jewelry box. He wasn't sure. If so, it wasn't very much space.

He pulled here, and he pushed there. If this thing opened up, it was like a puzzle box. He kept trying to move things, but with so much engraving, it was nearly impossible to see any cuts in the wood.

Desperate to figure this out so he could solve this case, he kept up his push/pull method. And then something shifted beneath his finger tip. It was a small strip of wood. His heart beat faster. This was it. He'd finally figured it out.

He pulled out the small slip of wood from beneath the lid and set it aside. Then he once more tried to open the top of the jewelry box. It didn't budge. He tried again with the same results. He expelled a frustrated groan.

There had to be another piece of wood locking the lid into place. He kept searching. At last, he found it. He removed the piece. This was it. The final step. He was certain of it.

He set aside the strip of wood and then he lifted on the lid of the jewelry box. This time it gave way. He moved it to the table and stared inside the hidden space. Inside were folded papers.

He withdrew them and unfolded them. They were bearer bonds. He didn't know much about them, but the amount on them and the number of them said they were valuable.

He heard movement at the top of the steps. Belle was coming. He still had his coat on so he stuffed the papers in the back of his jeans, then he replaced the top of the jewelry box. Thankfully, the two strips of wood quickly and easily slid into place.

The last piece of wood had just fallen into place when Belle entered the kitchen. She wore a worried frown on her face. He wanted to promise her that everything was going to work out, but he couldn't say that, because he didn't know how this situation was going to play, especially now that he knew the stakes were really high.

She stopped and stared at him as though she knew he was keeping something from her. "You figured it out, didn't you?"

He hesitated. Then knowing he couldn't lie to her, he explained what he'd found.

"Wow. I can't believe that was in the jewelry box. I probably never would have found them. Did you put them back?"

And this was why he didn't want to mention them to her. "No. And I'm not doing it."

"But you have to. If he knows they're gone, he won't give back Odie."

"We have no guarantee he'll give the dog back, even if he gets the bonds. The best thing to do is hang onto them so we have some leverage."

"I don't know..."

He glanced at the time on his phone. "Just trust me and go. You don't want to be late."

Belle slipped on her coat. When she reached for the jewelry box, she said, "Don't follow me."

He couldn't believe she didn't want his backup. She was either very brave or very desperate. He figured it was a little of both. But it didn't matter because she wasn't doing this alone. He got to his feet.

When he didn't say anything, she said, "Please. I'm begging you. Let's just do this part my way. I can't risk Odie."

Still, he said nothing because everything within him was screaming to stop her. But he knew by the determined look on her face that she was going to put up a fight, but it wouldn't stop him.

Buzz.

He reached for his phone. When he saw it was one of his deputies, he said, "Let me get this. It might be new information about the case."

She nodded.

He pressed the phone to his ear. "Bishop."

He didn't have a good connection. There was a lot of static on the line. He walked toward the kitchen because he had better reception there in the past.

He was in the process of pulling in every deputy he had to work this case. They had to be plain clothes. He didn't want to spook this guy. And then he and Stark worked out a plan to keep Belle safe and to get her dog back.

When he finished the call, he rushed back to tell Belle the plan, but she wasn't there. Thinking she might have gone upstairs to get something, he called up to her. There was no response.

And that's when he saw that the jewelry box was gone. He yanked open the front door. Her car wasn't in the driveway. She had gone without him.

His gut knotted with worry. He stepped into his boots before running out the door. With his phone pressed to his ear, he headed for his pickup.

Her phone rang and rang.

She didn't answer.

Belle knew it was Parker calling to yell at her for leaving without him. She wished he would understand that she had to do this. She had to do whatever it took to save Odie.

The ringing finally stopped. Silence once more filled the car. Belle expelled a sigh.

Buzz. Buzz.

Belle nearly jumped in her seat. She hadn't expected him to call back so quickly. She focused on the road and let the call go to voicemail.

She knew Parker would be angry with her. Still, she had to do this her way, erm...the dognapper's way. She wasn't going to lose someone else because she lied. It wasn't going to happen.

She desperately wanted her precious puppy back, safe and sound. At this hour on a snowy December evening, there wasn't anyone at the park.

She easily found a parking spot along the road. A glance at the clock on the dashboard let her know she was four minutes early. She stayed put as the warm air pumped out of the vents.

Her attention was on the occasional car that drove by. If they would slow down, her pulse raced. But once they passed the falls with its festive color display, they picked up speed, and she would sigh.

There was the occasional car that would slow down almost to a stop. Twice now they'd turned into a driveway across the street from the park. None of them were the dognapper. Where was he?

She squinted and stared into the dark. Was he already in the park? Her palms grew damp, and she rubbed them over her jeans. Was he watching her, and she didn't know it? Probably. Her breath came in short, fast gasps.

She looked for anyone walking in the park. There wasn't anyone on that below-freezing evening. She looked at the shadows to see if they moved. They didn't. But he had to be somewhere, and hopefully, Odie wasn't far away.

As she stared into the night, she knew she was letting her imagination get the best of her. She had to stay calm. She couldn't panic. Odie was relying on her to get this right. She drew in a deep breath and then slowly let it out. She repeated the process a few more times.

Buzz.

Her hand had a slight tremble to it as she grabbed up her phone from the passenger seat.

Her heart stilled as her chest tightened. Was it the dognapper with more instructions?

When she looked at the caller ID, she found it was Candi. Now wasn't the time for chit-chat. Belle sent the call to voicemail.

No sooner had she done that than the phone rang again. She lifted it to see if it was Candi calling back. It wasn't. It was Parker.

Her finger hovered over the answer button. She didn't want him to come rushing in and mess up the drop. She pressed the phone to her ear. "Parker, I need you to stay away. Nothing you say can stop me from doing this."

"Belle, just let me be there with you."

"No." She didn't need rescuing. "I've got this. Promise me that you'll stay away."

There was a tense silence. "Belle..."

"Parker, I'll be fine. Trust me." She disconnected the call. In frustration, she tossed the phone onto the passenger seat.

Her gaze moved back to the clock. The numbers glowed in the darkened interior of the car. She had two minutes until her drop off time. The problem was that she didn't know what happened after she made the drop. The dognapper better bring Odie with him, or there wouldn't be a deal.

Her gaze constantly moved through the park, looking for the dognapper and Odie. He had to bring Odie. As the clock got closer to her appointed time, the shivering in her stomach turned into a knot.

And then a car came down the road toward her. As she watched in the rearview mirror, her heart started to pound. Was this the man she was supposed to meet?

She couldn't see anything beyond the bright headlights. They were practically blinding. As the car drew closer, her heart beat faster.

And then they passed her by. They didn't even slow down. Her hopes were dashed.

She focused on the time again. One minute to go. It was time to make her move. Her insides were quivering with nerves as she opened the car door. She reached over for the jewelry box. It was pretty big and a little heavy. With the old jewelry box clutched to her chest, she got out of the car.

In the distance, she could hear singing. She wondered if the carolers were still out there, bringing smiles to so many people. She wished she was still with them because if she was, it would mean Odie was safe at home, and this was all just a terrible nightmare she could wake up from.

On wooden legs that didn't feel like her own, she started toward the waterfall. The snow had been cleared from the sidewalks. Putting one foot in front of the other, she kept repeating to herself: *Let Odie be okay. Let Odie be okay.*

There were a half dozen benches near the waterfall. She visually examined each one. All of them were snow-covered. It didn't stop her from searching for anything that might lead her to Odie. Her sweet puppy was nowhere in sight.

There wasn't even so much as a disturbance in the smooth coating of snow on each seat.

She didn't know which bench she was supposed to leave the jewelry box on. She picked the bench right in front of her. It was in the middle.

When she reached it, she wished she'd put on her snow gloves, but they were back in the car. Moving the jewelry box to her left arm, she used her right arm to brush the snow from the bench. All the while, she kept glancing over her shoulder to see if anyone was approaching her. She didn't see anyone.

What did she do next? Leave the jewelry box on the bench and walk away? *No.* She definitely wasn't doing that. She wasn't going to let this creep get away without giving her dog back.

Belle sat down on the bench. The coldness immediately seeped through her jeans. She didn't care. She was going to sit there until the guy showed his face.

Chapter Sixteen

He didn't like this.

Belle never should have gone off on her own.

Parker stood with a small group of carolers. Belle had never been truly alone. He'd called in help from the neighboring towns. He didn't have enough staff to cover the entire park.

He'd talked his mother into continuing the caroling on the other side of the street from the park. He wanted a distraction—something for the dognapper to focus on instead of him noticing Parker's people moving into position around the park.

As they walked down the sidewalk across from the park, he had his phone out. He was snapping photos of all the cars parked on the side of the street and those driving by. He would send them to the sheriff's office where they'd check the license plates for someone who didn't belong there. He was certain that whoever did this didn't live in Kringle Falls. Add in the fact that the estate auction where Belle bought the jewelry box was a couple of towns over only upped his suspicion that the suspect wasn't local.

Parker already had a couple of deputies situated in the park, out of sight. Everything within him wanted to run to Belle's side. He couldn't believe she'd taken off on her own. When he saw her again, he was going to hug her, and then he was going to have a big talk with her about safety. Then he was going to hug her again.

All she had to do was place the jewelry box on the bench and walk away. He could see her from where he stood across the road. At least she'd picked the bench under one of the lights. He wanted to be a lot closer, but he didn't know how to do that without alerting the suspect.

So far, all of the cars he'd checked out were empty, and the plates checked out. These cars were all where they were supposed to be. It made him start to doubt his suspicions about the suspect. Was it possible it was a Kringle Falls resident?

And then movement out of the corner of his eye caught his attention. He turned his head to see a dark figure walking a dog through the park. The breath stilled in his lungs. This was it.

He lifted his phone to his ear. "Everyone be ready to move. The subject is approaching Belle."

While the carolers kept walking, he stopped on the sidewalk. He stared at the scene unfolding in front of him. The dog seemed large, nothing like the photos of Odie that Belle had displayed around the house.

When the subject reached the bench Belle was sitting on, he didn't so much as pause. He kept going. It was a false alarm. Parker struggled to keep the frustration from his voice as he spoke into his phone. "False alarm."

Knowing he couldn't continue to stand there on the sidewalk all by himself, staring at Belle, he turned and took long, fast steps to catch up with the carolers. They were going to walk to the end of the next block and then retrace their steps. He was so appreciative to his mother for making this happen. He was going to have to figure out a special way to thank her.

He wanted to continue to stare at Belle, but if the subject was around, he couldn't give himself away. He had to have faith in the people he had in the park who were watching over her. This whole event wasn't going to be over soon enough for him.

When he rejoined the carolers, his mother leaned toward him. "Is everything all right?"

He nodded. Though everything inside him said that nothing was right—not with Belle being a sitting duck for this unpredictable suspect.

The longer she sat there, the colder she became.

At first glance, Belle had thought for certain the person walking their dog had been the suspect. But as they'd gotten closer, she realized the dog was too big to be Odie. Disappointment settled in her chest.

The breeze picked up, grabbing the top layer of snow and tossing it around. The icy flakes smacked her in the face as the frigid air hit her lungs. It was so cold out and yet, she wasn't going anywhere.

She turned her head left and right but she didn't see anyone. No one wanted to be out on such a cold evening—except for the carolers. She couldn't remember them mentioning coming to this part of town. Still, the sound of their voices gave her hope that somehow this mess was going to work out.

Her thoughts turned back to Parker. She was so appreciative of him for staying away. She knew he didn't want to do it, but it was for the best. Secretly, as the time had dragged on, she started to think she was never going to be reunited with Odie. But then the dognapper had called, and now they were so close to being together again.

Belle rubbed her bare hands together. She couldn't believe she'd forgotten her gloves. She was apparently more nervous about this meeting than she'd let on to herself.

If one good thing had to come out of this event, it was that she was able to see Parker in a different light. He was a really good guy—even if he clung to the rules a little too tightly. But give her some time, and she'd have him seeing shades of gray instead of everything being black and white.

Wee-oow. Wee-oow.

Belle's head turned in the direction of the sirens and lights. Two police cars pulled to a stop at the edge of the park. What were they doing?

Her heart sank. The dognapper was never going to show with law enforcement there. More law enforcement vehicles rolled up on the scene. Whatever was going on was a big deal.

And then she realized she'd forgotten her phone in the car too. What if the guy had called her to change plans? A feeling of dread settled in her stomach.

She got up from the bench, grabbed the jewelry box, and headed back to her car. She was just steps from her car when Parker approached her.

She frowned at him. "What are you doing here? I told you to let me handle this."

He straightened his shoulders. "We arrested him."

"What?" Had she heard him correctly?

"We arrested the suspect." He gestured toward all of the flashing lights. "You don't have to worry anymore."

"But how do you know it's him?"

"When we ran the plates, there's a BOLO (be-on-the-lookout) for the car and there's a bench warrant out for him. Long story short, he was left out of his family's will. Instead of settling it in court, he's decided to take what he thinks he deserves."

Her gaze searched his. "It's really over?"

He smiled and nodded. "It is. And you're safe."

"And Odie? Is he in the car?" Her gaze searched his.

"I don't know. I'm just about to go get briefed on everything."

"Let's go." She turned to walk toward the commotion.

Parker reached out, catching her upper arm. "Not so fast."

"I have to get to Odie."

"First, we have to turn over the jewelry box for evidence."

"Oh. Yes." Her thoughts were utterly scattered.

Once the jewelry box was handed over to the deputy, they walked toward the scene. While Parker talked to his people, Belle wasn't able to get close to the suspect's car. It didn't stop her from squinting to see if there was a dog inside. It didn't appear that Odie was in the car. She glanced around to see if someone had gotten him out. She didn't see any sign of Odie. But he had to be somewhere.

She approached a uniformed officer. "Excuse me. Was there a dog in the car?"

The older guy looked at her with sympathy in his eyes and shook his head. "I didn't see one."

She wasn't willing to accept that answer, because if it were true—if Odie wasn't there—then... She refused to continue that line of thought.

She moved to the next person and inquired about Odie. They hadn't seen him either. She didn't stop. She kept asking anyone and everyone. Someone had to have seen him, right?

Parker approached her. The solemn look on his face made her blood chill. Before he could get a word out, she said, "What? Where is he?"

He reached out to her, but she backed up out of his reach. "He said he doesn't have Odie."

"Then he's the wrong guy. You arrested the wrong guy." Her mind raced as she figured out what this meant. "What if the dognapper is here...watching us?"

"Belle, this is the right guy. He had pictures of your house and of you at work. They were in his car."

"But... But where is Odie?"

"I don't know yet."

"Well, ask him. Where is he? I'll ask him." She turned around, looking for the police vehicle with the dognapper in the back.

"Belle, he's not here. They already left with him."

She swung around and glared at Parker. "How could you let him leave without telling us where Odie is?"

"Trust me, it's going to be my first question. We will get an answer. But right now, I need you to go home."

She shook her head. "I'm not going home. I'm going with you."

"You can't. This is official business."

"But..."

"No, Belle. I'm sorry. But you can't be there. I called Michael and Candi." He pointed to them approaching. "They were in town and said they'd be happy to wait with you."

Before she could vocalize her protest, her friends were within earshot, and she wasn't going to say anything to hurt their feelings. She felt so helpless and scared that she might never see Odie again.

How had this all gone so wrong? And then she realized if the police hadn't intervened, the dognapper would have taken the jewelry box, and she still wouldn't have Odie. Unless...

Her gaze strayed to the car. Dread filled her but she had to ask. "Did... Did you check the trunk?"

Sympathy shone in Parker's eyes. "Yes. He wasn't there."

"Then where is he?"

"We'll find him. I promise. Just go home. I'll call as soon as we have something."

Candi rushed over to her and put her arm around her shoulders. "Hey, how are you doing?"

Belle didn't have an answer to that question. So, she shrugged.

In the end, she drove her Jeep home with Candi next to her while Michael trailed behind them. She just couldn't help thinking that if Parker had done as she'd asked, that the dognapper would have told her where to find Odie. Why didn't Parker trust her?

Chapter Seventeen

She was angry, and he couldn't blame her.

This hadn't gone the way either of them had hoped.

Parker had talked to the suspect. The first question he asked him was where was Odie. The suspect refused to answer. After trying again and again, Parker moved on to other questions.

Finally, the suspect opened up about his motivation for taking Belle's dog and vandalizing her house. It seemed the suspect felt he'd been cheated out of his portion of the family estate. The suspect also knew about a secret his father had told him many years ago—back before he was kicked out of the will.

After his father's death, the family had been searching for those bearer bonds but couldn't find them. It appeared when their father got on in years that he got eccentric. He hid lots of things, including all of the flatware, which made eating difficult. They had to buy him plastic flatware. He hid those as well.

Parker tried again to get the guy to divulge what he'd done with Odie, but he refused to speak of the dog. It gave Parker an uneasy feeling in his gut.

When his phone rang, and it was Belle, he let it go to voicemail. He just couldn't tell her that they still had no idea where her beloved dog was. He had some more digging to do before he was willing to give her that news.

Next, they executed a search warrant on the suspect's house. Parker was there. He didn't know what he expected to find. The place was a small white bungalow. The outside appeared to be in disrepair with peeling paint and torn screens on the windows.

Once inside, Parker found the interior of the home dirty and unkempt. There were dirty dishes piled in the sink, and the trash was overflowing. Parker found himself gagging more than once. This was bad, really bad.

"Back here," Deputy Williams called out.

Parker stepped toward the back of the small house. There was a bathroom straight ahead with a bedroom on either side. He glanced to the left and then the right, where he spotted Williams.

When he stepped up to the doorway of the bedroom, he couldn't believe what he was seeing. Odie was there being fussed over by another deputy. He breathed a sigh of relief. He couldn't wait to tell Belle. He knew how worried she was about Odie.

His gaze continued to move about the room, and that was when he noticed the room was clean. There was a dog bed, little pastel blankets, and dog toys. This room conflicted with the rest of the house. It made no sense.

"Can you believe this?" Williams asked. "It doesn't look like the man had any intention of giving Odie back. I mean, look at that basket full of toys." Williams leaned down and picked up one of the toys. "It's a hedgehog."

Williams gave the toy a squeeze. The hedgehog let out a loud squeak. Odie ran over and started jumping for the toy. Williams gave it to him. The pup ran around the room with it in his mouth and his tail wagging.

"Can you find a leash?" Parker asked. "I have to make a call, and then I'm taking him home."

"What about the house?" Williams asked.

"You're in charge of the search. Make sure nothing is overlooked."

"Yes, sir."

Parker stepped out of the house and drew in some fresh air. He pulled up Belle's number and then pressed the phone to his ear. The phone rang only once before Belle came on the line.

"Did you find Odie? Is he okay?"

"We found him. And yes, he's okay. He misses you."

"He..." Her voice cracked. "He's really okay?"

"Yes, he is." There was a pause, and Parker imagined her with tears of joy.

"Where is he?" she asked. "I want to come get him."

"I'm bringing him to you."

"I can't wait. Please. Tell me where you are."

"I'm going to scoop him up and head to you right now."

"Oh. Okay. I'll see you soon."

Parker was smiling by the time he slipped the phone back into his pocket. Finally, Belle was going to have her happily ever after, with the dog of course. But at last, the time was right for him to officially ask her out.

—ℓℓ—

She was so excited.

And yet she wouldn't let that excitement out.

Belle paced back and forth in her house. She'd sent Candi and Michael home a while ago, promising she'd be fine. They didn't want to go, but they understood she just wanted a little time alone. They told her to call if she needed anything. The only thing she needed was her puppy and Parker was bringing him to her.

She wanted to smile and squeal with excitement, but she couldn't let herself. She was afraid of jinxing it. She remembered her parents' car accident. When the deputy had taken such pains to hold back the bad news, she immediately jumped to the conclusion that both of her parents were alive and well.

When they reached the hospital, and she was told her father had passed, it felt like someone had pulled the rug out from under her. She tried but she couldn't get her footing after that. It always felt as though everything was off kilter.

When they informed her that her mother was still hanging in there, she'd clung to that news like it was a life preserver. She couldn't deal with the loss of her father, so she'd pinned all of her hopes on her mother surviving. So much so that she didn't hear the cautions the doctors issued with each update.

And then later that night, she'd fallen asleep in the waiting area. She had been jostled awake to find out that she'd lost not just one parent but both of them. The pain was just too much. She'd closed off her heart after her entire world had been upended. To this day, she remained guarded.

Well, that wasn't quite true. When Odie entered her life, everything changed. She didn't know how to explain it. They'd clicked at first sight. It was like they were meant to be.

He peeled back the protective wall around her scarred heart and snuggled in. He was the one that opened her eyes to see how much she missed by keeping everyone at arm's length.

Thankfully, the little guy was on his way home. She should plug in the Christmas tree because he liked the little lights, but she didn't do it. She should put his favorite blanket on the couch, but she didn't do it either.

She couldn't let herself believe that Odie was truly coming home because if he didn't—if something happened—it would crush her just like it had on that long ago night at the hospital. She wouldn't let herself celebrate until she held Odie in her arms and saw with her own eyes he was all right.

Instead, she paced and waited. And then she heard a vehicle pull into the driveway. She slipped on her boots before yanking open the front door. She rushed out onto the porch and spotted Parker's pickup.

Odie is home!

Her heart leaped with glee. She ran off the porch and headed straight for the pickup. Parker got out and rounded the front of the pickup. In that moment, her gaze was laser-focused on the passenger's seat. When she got closer, she saw Odie. His tail was wagging about a million swishes a minute. The wags were so intense his whole backside moved with his tail.

Happy tears blurred her vision as she reached for the door handle at the same time as Parker. His warm hand wrapped over hers. She blinked back the tears and looked at him. Her heart lodged in her throat. In that moment, she didn't have the words to tell him how much this meant to her.

Odie barked and pawed the window, pulling her attention away from Parker. She pulled her hand away from Parker's touch.

"Let me get the door for you." He moved off to the side. "Are you ready?"

A big smile pulled at her lips. She was so ready for this. "Yes."

Parker opened the door, and then Odie leaped into her arms. He lathered her with puppy kisses. She closed her eyes and let the puppy shower her with love.

It was only then that the fear she'd been holding back hit her. Tears rushed to her eyes, and she hugged Odie close. With the light snowflakes fluttering through the night sky, they stood there. She didn't know how much time passed as she hugged Odie.

"I love you," she whispered.

She pulled herself together and carried Odie into the house. When he saw the basket with his toys in it, he wiggled to get down. She put him on the floor. He started sniffing everything. He explored each room as though making sure nothing had changed during his absence.

She stepped over to Parker. When her gaze met his, her heart tumbled in her chest. "Thank you."

He nodded. "Looks like he's happy to be home."

She glanced over at Odie as he nosed his way through his toys. "I missed him so much."

"He missed you too."

She was hesitant to ask but she had to know. "Were they mean to him?"

"You will be relieved to know that he was well taken care of."

"Really?" She had a hard time believing it after her imagination betrayed her and conjured up so many horrific scenarios.

Parker nodded. "He was all set up in a bedroom with toys and blankets."

"But I don't understand. Why would this guy do that?"

Parker paused, as though weighing what to say to her. "I think he was planning to keep Odie."

Belle gasped. Her gaze moved to the puppy as he grabbed his green squeaky alligator. *Squeak. Squeak. Squeak.*

She had been right to worry about not seeing him again. But she was thankful that Odie had been well-cared for. She couldn't really have asked for more.

There was a part of her that wanted to shut down her emotions—to not love the little puppy with her whole heart—because she knew too well the total devastation of losing someone whom she loved. She didn't want to feel that sort of pain again.

Odie meandered over to the Christmas tree. He nosed at the lower limbs of the pine tree. He was probably searching for an ornament to steal. He thought it was a fun game. She did not.

But since the debacle with the Christmas tree, there weren't many ornaments left, so there were none in the vicinity of the puppy. He continued to walk around the tree.

She walked over and plugged in the lights. She knelt down and pet Odie. "I'm so glad you're home. I missed you."

He placed his paws on her legs, lifted himself up, and then licked her face. Was that his way of telling her that he missed her too?

Odie moved away, and Belle straightened. She stepped back and watched as the puppy walked around and then found the perfect spot to lie down under the tree. It was like he was her Christmas present. He was the most perfect gift.

Parker stepped up behind her and wrapped his arms around her. In that moment, everything felt right in this world. She leaned her head back against Parker's chest. She closed her eyes and just let herself be present in this moment. This perfect, wonderful moment.

When Parker moved his arms, a great disappointment came over her. She didn't want this precious moment to end. She had everything she wanted right here—right now. Her heart was full.

His hands gently gripped her shoulders. He prodded her to turn around. She wondered what he wanted. When she turned, he wrapped his arms around her waist and stared into her eyes.

He lowered his head and pressed his lips to hers. Belle didn't move. He had caught her off-guard. Her heart leaped into her throat. But as his lips moved over hers, she lost her train of thought. The only thing she could think about was that she'd never been kissed like this before.

She kissed him back. As the kiss intensified, she felt as though her feet had left the floor. It was as if they were floating on cloud nine.

Her hands slid from his chest up over his broad shoulders and then snaked around the back of his neck. Her heart pounded in her chest. He was a really good guy—the best.

If something happened to him—if he left her—she wouldn't make it through it. The scars on her heart ached. Because she never got over the premature loss of her parents. She learned to live with the pain—the gaping hole in her heart. But she didn't ever get over having her life torn apart at eighteen.

But with Parker—she didn't think his loss would be something she could learn to live with. It would kill her. Maybe not literally, but it would kill a part of her, and she would never be the same again.

Therefore, she couldn't fall for him. But she couldn't hide from the truth. It was right there in his kiss. It was in the beating of her heart.

I love Parker.

Fear caused her heart to still. *No. This isn't happening.*

She pulled out of his embrace. She couldn't think clearly when he was touching her. She took a step back. She expelled a pent-up breath as her heart resumed beating.

The cold fingers of fear wrapped around her chest, making it hard to breathe. It froze the joyous feelings ricocheting around in her chest.

This thing—this very special thing she had with Parker—it couldn't happen. She couldn't give him her heart, because the risk was too great. Because she couldn't go through the dark days of agony—the long days of piecing herself back together and trying to compensate for the cracks in her heart that would never go away.

Parker sent her a confused look. "What's wrong?"

"This. You and me. I..." Her breathing was quick, and her hands felt jittery. "I can't do this."

"Can't do what?" His gaze penetrated her, as though he were searching for the answer.

"I told you...you and me." Her voice cracked with emotion. She swallowed hard, trying to tuck away her internal turmoil. "You can't care for me." *Wait. That didn't come out right.* "I mean, I can't care about you."

His brows drew together. "Why not?"

This was not how she anticipated this conversation going. She thought he'd get angry and storm out the door. But he wasn't making any motion to leave. And now he expected an explanation.

She shook her head. "Parker, just go."

"I don't want to go. I want to figure out why you're pushing me away. Talk to me. Because I know you have feelings for me." There was a certainty to his voice.

She inwardly groaned as her gaze moved to the floor. Either she was doing this all wrong, or he was unlike any of the guys she'd broken up with in the past.

She drew in a deep breath, trying to calm herself, but it wasn't working. This was the hardest thing she'd done. "Parker, thank you for bringing Odie back to me, but whatever we had, it...it's over. I want you to leave. Now."

She hated how she'd sounded so harsh. It was the last thing she wanted to do, but it was better now than later. She didn't do long-term relationships. And she wasn't going to change that for Parker. She refused to treat him differently. Nothing good would come of it.

When she raised her gaze to meet his, she knew she'd made a mistake by looking at him. She saw the pain in his eyes. The hurt that she'd inflicted upon him. It added to the guilt that was threatening to smother her.

He stood there for the longest moment, staring at her with those pain-filled eyes. Her heart ached. She assured herself that this pain was less than the pain she'd feel if she were to commit herself to him and then lose him—after all, he was the sheriff. It was a dangerous job.

And then without a word, he turned and walked out the door. When he closed the door, it wasn't slammed shut. Instead, it soundlessly closed, except for the snick of the latch.

And then she was alone, except for Odie. She stood there until she heard the pickup start and then the sound of the engine gradually faded away.

By then, the tears she'd been holding in spilled onto her cheeks. She moved to the couch and sank down onto the cushion. No sooner had she sat down than Odie jumped up next to her. He wiggled onto her lap.

She wrapped her arms around him and held him to her chest. Her head rested on his. And she let her emotions pour out. She'd only been this scared one other time in her life, and that was the night her parents died.

Parker kept filling her every thought. She already missed him. But this was for the best. It wouldn't have lasted—love never did. Telling herself this did nothing to make her feel better. She still felt horrible—like she'd just lost the best thing in her life.

Chapter Eighteen

Where had everything gone so wrong?

Even after a sleepless night, he didn't have any answers.

The next day, Parker returned to work. He was thankful he had something to do. If he was at home, his thoughts would do nothing but torture him.

He couldn't figure out how things had gone so wrong with Belle. One moment she was thanking him for bringing Odie back to her, and the next thing he knew, she was saying things were over.

Maybe it was just the stress over Odie catching up with her. Maybe a good night's sleep would have her seeing things differently. He could only hope.

He reached for his phone, and before he could talk himself out of it, he called her. The phone rang and rang. Then it switched to voicemail. Instead of leaving a message, he hung up.

He thought of going to see her, but he didn't let himself. He knew from experience that even if the relationship was working for one person, that didn't mean it was working for the other person.

He thought they had finally worked past all of the contention from their past. But apparently Belle didn't feel the same way. How could he have been so wrong about them?

When he glanced at the dashboard, he noticed it was seven forty. There were four vehicles lined up at the red light. He made it five vehicles. It was what constituted rush hour in Kringle Falls. When he cleared the intersection, he drove a little farther and then turned around. He maneuvered his official SUV into his position on the edge of town to wait for speeders.

As he watched car after car pass by, none of them were Belle. Had she changed things up from her usual drive to work? She could be trying to avoid him. Or had she called off from work? It would make sense that she was wiped out after everything she'd gone through.

And then a worrisome thought came to mind. Was something wrong with Odie?

He halted his rambling thoughts. He told himself it was the lack of sleep that had his mind working in overdrive, but he couldn't shake the feeling that something was wrong. He checked the time. It was now seven fifty-six. His brother Colin's office didn't open until nine.

Parker reached for his phone and dialed his brother's cell phone. Colin answered on the second ring. "Hey. I wasn't expecting to hear from you this morning. Is everything all right?"

"I don't know," Parker said in all honesty.

There was a pause. "Well, then why did you call?"

"I was wondering if you could make a house call."

"You mean to check in on Odie?"

Parker nodded and then he realized his brother couldn't see him. "Yes. I don't think Belle went to work today, and I'm worried that I was too quick to assume nothing was wrong with the puppy. Could you go check on them?"

"Isn't that something you should do?"

Parker's jaw tightened. He really didn't want to get into this, but his brother wasn't leaving him much choice. "Things...uh, aren't going well between Belle and me."

"Really? You two seemed really close the last time I saw you."

Seriously? He was going to make him talk about this. "She told me things were over."

"Ouch. Yeah. I'd agree that things aren't going well. What did you do wrong?"

"Me?" Actually, it was the same question he'd asked himself last night while he'd been staring into the darkness of his bedroom. He never did come up with an answer. But he didn't like his brother jumping to the conclusion that it was his fault. Even if he was most likely right. "Why do you think it's my fault?"

"As the big brother, you do have a tendency to take control of the situation and boss people around."

"I do not." The denial flew out of his mouth. He only did that when his younger brothers were acting careless. But had he done that with Belle? He didn't think so.

"You still do it once in a while."

Parker really wanted to argue the point, but he had a feeling his brother might be right. But was that the problem with Belle? Was she upset about him insisting on going with her to meet the suspect? But she hadn't let his words stop her; she'd taken off on her own.

Trying to unravel what went wrong between them was giving him a headache. "I need to get back to work. Could you just stop over and check in on Odie? I'd really appreciate it."

"I can do that. I was just heading out the door. I'll head over now. Are you going to let her know I'm coming?"

He thought of how his earlier phone call had gone to voicemail. "No. It's probably best if you just show up."

"Uh...okay. Should I tell her that you sent me?"

"No." The answer came out faster than he would have liked.

After the call ended, Parker stared at his phone as he debated calling her. But he kept hearing her saying the thing between them was over. Funny thing was that he'd thought their story had just been getting started. How did he convince her of that?

She'd called off work.

Belle just wasn't ready to leave Odie. He'd been glued to her side since Parker had brought him home. He seemed really happy to be back, but he wasn't eating much. It had her worried, and that was why she'd finally made the decision to stay home.

They needed the day to hang out together and unwind. The prior week had been so stressful for the both of them. Odie couldn't tell her what he'd been through, but she worried that he was traumatized.

Her boss, Mavis, had been understanding and told her to get some rest. Belle planned to do exactly that. She had a bunch of holiday movies recorded. With the snow lightly falling, it was the perfect day to curl up on the couch beneath a blanket, and with Odie by her side, she'd watch some Christmas movies.

After she tried to get Odie to eat again and failed, the pup jumped onto the couch. He settled himself in the middle of the blanket. Belle smiled and shook her head. For a little fellow, he was always stealing the blankets.

She went back to the kitchen to make herself a tall mug of hot coffee with lots of milk. She was carrying it to the living room when she heard a knock at the door. It startled her. She wasn't expecting anyone. And then she thought it might be Parker.

He'd called earlier while she was outside with Odie. He hadn't left a message. She thought of calling him back, but she knew if it was important, he would call back. Maybe instead of calling back, he'd decided to see her in person.

Odie started barking at the top of his little lungs and charged toward the door. Belle put her coffee down and followed him to the door. She owed Parker an apology for the way she abruptly ended things. It hadn't been her finest moment.

As Odie continued to bark, she picked him up. "Hush."

Odie pretended not to hear her and continued to bark.

With a sigh, she opened the door. Her apology for Parker was on the tip of her tongue. When she found her visitor was Colin, she stumbled over her greeting. "Oh. Hi." And then gathering her thoughts, she opened the door farther. "Don't mind the yappy one. He thinks he's a guard dog. Come on in out of the snow."

Colin stepped inside. "Sorry to just stop by."

"No problem." She wondered why he was there. And then it came to her. "If you're looking for Parker, he's not here."

"That's okay. I'm not here to see him." He held up his doctor's bag. And then he turned to Odie, who was wagging his tail. "Hello."

Colin cautiously held out his hand for Odie to sniff. Once Odie seemed fine with him, he reached out and pet him. Thankfully, it quieted him down.

Colin lowered his arm. "I heard about Odie, and I wanted to check in on him."

"I didn't know you did house calls."

"I don't. But this is a special circumstance."

That was putting it mildly. Still, she thought there was more to his visit than him just going out of his way for one of his patients.

Although, he had really good timing. "I was actually going to call your office when it opened."

Colin's eyes widened. "Is something wrong?"

"I can't get Odie to eat much. He'll eat a couple bites of food, and then he walks away. That's not like him. He used to always wolf down his food. I had to buy him a slow feeder bowl, but now he doesn't have much of an appetite. And his stomach is upset." She went on to lay out the details.

Colin nodded his head. "Is he drinking?"

"Yes."

"That's a good sign. Do you mind if I examine him?"

"Sure. Go ahead. I would really appreciate it. I took today off from work because I just didn't think he was up for staying home alone."

She carried Odie into the living room. Colin was very gentle with Odie as he examined him. He didn't rush through the exam. He took the time to talk to her and ask questions about how long Odie was gone and how he reacted when he got home.

She wrung her hands together as she waited for Colin's verdict. Was there something wrong with Odie? She hoped not.

At last, Colin straightened. He sent her a reassuring smile. "I think Odie has been through a lot over the past week. He needs a bit to adjust to being home. I checked him all out, and it appears the person that had him took care of him."

She nodded. "That's what Parker told me. He thought the person was planning to keep Odie."

"I see." Colin was quiet for a moment as though not sure what to say. "As long as he's drinking and eating a little bit, I wouldn't worry for a couple of days. I think once he relaxes that his appetite will come back. But if it doesn't, call my office, and we'll see what's going on."

Belle breathed easier. "Thanks so much for stopping over. It's a relief to hear that he's all right."

"I'm glad this story had a happy ending."

"Me too." She felt the need to give credit where credit was due. "Parker was really great through this whole sordid affair. He went above and beyond. I really appreciate him bringing Odie back to me."

Colin arched a brow. "He had a lot of good things to say about you too."

Heat rushed to her cheeks. "He did?"

Colin nodded. "I'm not supposed to tell you, but it was Parker's idea for me to come over this morning."

Belle was touched by Parker's thoughtfulness. She started to wonder if she'd made a huge mistake by ending things with him. She'd been reacting in the moment, and perhaps she let her exhaustion and emotions get the best of her.

Chapter Nineteen

SHE STILL HADN'T CALLED.

Late Tuesday afternoon, Parker got off work and headed home. The house was quiet—too quiet. After his engagement ended, he'd prided himself on being a bachelor. He made peace with his solitary existence.

But after spending time with Belle, he realized he preferred to share his life with someone—not just someone but with Belle. There was something about her that brought happiness to his life—a reason to hit the ground running in the morning. And now he didn't know what to do to win her back.

He was hoping after she calmed down and Odie settled back in that she would realize they really did belong together. But so far, she still hadn't called him. And it was taking all of his self-restraint not to call her again.

And so, on the way home, he might have stopped by Kringle Blooms and ordered a bouquet of red and white roses to be delivered to Belle. But since it was so late in the day, they couldn't deliver them until the following day. He agreed and instructed them to deliver the flowers to Frills & Heels. When they asked if he wanted to fill out a card to go with the flowers, he'd declined. He wasn't sure what to write.

And now he wondered if he'd made a mistake. Were the flowers too forward? Should he just cease all contact? He wasn't sure. He didn't want to make things worse.

Knock-knock.

Before Parker could answer, the door flung open. "Hey, Parker, you here?"

He recognized his brother's voice. "In the kitchen."

Stomp-stomp.

Michael appeared in the entrance of the kitchen. "Did you just get home?" When Parker nodded, Michael said, "Mom's been trying to get a hold of you."

Parker knew it. He'd been avoiding his family because he didn't know what to say to them about Belle. He couldn't explain to them what had happened between them because he didn't understand it himself.

"I've, uh, been busy," Parker said. "I just haven't had a chance to call her back."

He knew that if it was anything urgent, one of his brothers would track him down. His family was close that way.

Michael nodded. "So, you're avoiding her."

Parker opened his mouth to deny the allegation, but he knew it was pointless. He wordlessly pressed his lips together and shrugged.

Michael nodded in understanding. "She wanted to know if you're bringing Belle to Christmas dinner."

"Why would I do that?"

"Because it's obvious to everyone that you're crazy about her. And I think she's crazy about you too."

He shook his head. "I don't think so."

"Why?"

He really didn't want to talk about it, but he knew his brother wouldn't let the subject drop until he told him. "She dumped me."

Michael's eyes widened. "Man, I'm sorry. But are you sure?"

He glared at his brother. "Of course, I'm sure. I think I'm smart enough to know when someone doesn't want to see me anymore."

"So, what are you doing about it?"

He thought about the flowers he'd ordered but decided it was best not to mention them. "Nothing. Okay. If I didn't have bad luck with women, then I wouldn't have any luck at all."

"If you're really into her, don't give up. You know it wasn't easy for me with Candi. After losing Evelyn and Noah, I didn't think I would ever be open to another serious relationship. And then Candi crashed into my life, literally. I did everything to fight the thing that was growing between us. Thankfully, Candi never gave up on me. Well, I guess she eventually did give up, but by then I got my head screwed on straight."

Parker shook his head. "But that was different. You lost your family."

"And Belle lost her family. It might have been years ago, but no one in Kringle will forget that tragedy. I don't know if there was a dry eye in that funeral home. Don't you remember? They couldn't even fit everyone in there. Belle was still a teenager. That loss must have left its scars on her. Maybe she just needs you to go slow."

"For once, you're making some sense." He never thought of it that way. And then he recalled her reaction to the Christmas ornaments being shattered. Speaking of which...

After his brother left, Parker retrieved the box of broken ornaments from his pickup. He couldn't just throw them out. They meant too much to Belle. He just needed to figure out a way to present them to her again.

The house was quiet...too quiet.

And work was too busy.

Wednesday evening, when Belle got home from work, Odie didn't meet her at the door like he normally did. After taking off her boots and shrugging off her coat, she found him waking up on the couch. When he saw her, his little tail started thumping against the couch.

He was eating again, but he still wasn't himself. It was like he didn't sleep the whole time he was gone, and he was just now catching up on it.

She scooped Odie up in her arms. His head rested on her shoulder. Belle snuggled him. His warm little body fit perfectly in her arms. Her heart swelled.

"I love you, little one," she whispered in his ear.

She carried him over and plugged in the Christmas tree lights. She settled on the couch and pet Odie. Her gaze strayed to the vase of red and white roses. They'd been delivered to the boutique the day before, but they still looked just as fresh as the moment they'd been handed to her.

There hadn't been a card with them. But she didn't need a card to know they were from Parker. She wondered why he'd go to the effort of sending her flowers but wouldn't include a message. It certainly had her puzzled. After what she'd said to him, why would he send her roses?

A few minutes later, Odie got off her lap and settled on the couch next to her. His body pressed against her thigh. Life was getting back to normal. So, then, why did she feel as though something was missing?

Buzz.

When she got up from the couch, Odie let out a little whimper. She looked back at him. "It's okay, little one. I'll be right back."

She grabbed her purse from next to the door. She reached inside and quickly found her phone. She glanced at the screen and found it was Merry Kringle. She wondered why she was calling. Maybe she wanted to check in on Odie. After all, it was Merry who brought Odie into her life. She owed the woman a debt of gratitude.

Belle pressed the phone to her ear as she retraced her steps back to the couch. "Hello."

"Oh, hi, Belle. You didn't leave yet, did you?" Without waiting for a response, she rushed on. "I forgot the pretzel sticks. Is there any chance you could pick up a half dozen bags or so?"

Pretzel sticks? Belle didn't know what she was talking about. Lately, her mind had been filled with thoughts of Parker. And wondering if she'd made the right decision.

"Belle? Did you hear me?" Merry's voice drew Belle's attention.

"Uh, yes."

"I'm sorry to call on you. But I'm already here at the community center setting up for the competition."

And then it dawned on Belle. Tonight was the gingerbread house competition. This wasn't one of those dramatic competitions like they had on television with the three- and four-feet tall structures. This contest was modest in comparison.

"So, you'll pick up the pretzels?" Merry asked.

Belle didn't want to go out. She didn't want to be around a bunch of cheerful partygoers. But she couldn't turn down Merry. "Yes, I will. I'll be there shortly. I just need to change clothes and get Odie some dinner."

"How is the little guy doing? It was so horrible what happened to the two of you."

"He's doing better every day. It's like he was on alert the whole time he was gone, just waiting for me to come get him. And now that he's home, he's wiped out."

"It'll take him a bit, but I'm sure he'll feel safe and secure again. It was great that Parker was there to help you bring him home."

He was the last person she wanted to talk about. "Yes. He was great."

"You two spent a lot of time together. I heard he stayed at your place to protect you. That's so chivalrous."

Belle inwardly groaned. She didn't want to think about how awesome Parker was, because it made her regret how she'd ended things between them.

Anxious to end this line of conversation, Belle said, "I better get going if I'm going to pick up the pretzel sticks. I'll see you in a little bit."

"Looking forward to it."

Belle disconnected the call and looked at Odie. His eyes opened, and he yawned. He stretched and then found a new position to go back to sleep. "Must be nice."

After putting some food out for him, she changed into a red sweater and a pair of blue jeans. She would pick up the pretzel sticks and drop them off at the community center, but as soon as she was done, she was leaving.

Chapter Twenty

His idea was taking shape.

Parker looked down at the polished pieces of colored glass. He'd used an old rock tumbler he'd found in his parents' garage to smooth out the sharp edges. He wished it was as easy to smooth out his relationship with Belle.

He'd been working every evening on this project. He intended to make something special out of broken ornaments. He'd bought clear glass ornaments and a low-heat glue gun. After sanding the glass to roughen up the surface for better adhesion, he'd adhered various shaped bits of colored glass to the ornament.

He wanted the ornaments to be perfect for Belle. He wanted to pay homage to the heirloom ornaments that once graced Belle's tree.

Knowing it would be impossible to cover the entire ornament in glass fragments, he'd gone to the craft store to buy fine white glitter glue. He used it like sparkly grout between the shards of glass.

He'd been working on the project every chance he had. At last, he was working on the final ornament. He only had a few more pieces of glass to glue to the ornament. He picked up a green bit of glass and, using the glue gun, he dabbed some glue on the base and then pressed the green glass to it. He held it for a few seconds to make sure the glue took hold.

He just set the ornament down in order to choose another piece of polished glass when his phone rang. It was probably work. He was used to them calling him after hours with questions. To him, being the sheriff wasn't a nine to five job. It was a way of life. And he loved what he did.

He put his phone on speaker as he worked to clean up the annoying glue strands. "Bishop."

"Parker, is that you?" a female voice asked.

"Yes. Who is this?"

"Oh, sorry. It's Merry Kringle."

"Hello, Mrs. Kringle. What can I do for you?"

"We have a problem, and we need your help."

He stopped cleaning up his mess. Suddenly, he slipped into his sheriff persona. He picked up the phone and pressed it to his ear. "Did you call nine-one-one?"

"Uh, no. It's not that serious."

He sighed in relief. "But you need me?"

"Yes. Please."

He couldn't imagine what she wanted his assistance for if it had nothing to do with his sheriff duties. "Could you tell me what this pertains to?"

"Uh..." It sounded like someone was speaking to her in the background, but the voices were muffled, as though the phone was covered. "Parker,

I have to go. If you could come to the community center right away, I would greatly appreciate it." And then the phone went dead.

He lowered his phone. The community center? It took him a moment to remember, but there was a Christmas event taking place there that evening. What in the world had gone wrong that they would need him?

With a sigh, he unplugged the glue gun. He only had a few more pieces of glass to attach to the last ornament. He would work on it when he got back. He still had to add the glitter glue and then seal them. He would have to keep at it since Christmas was just a couple days away.

Just in and out.

That was Belle's plan when she arrived at the community center. Sure, she'd signed up for the gingerbread house competition, but that had been before the dognapping and before she'd ruined things between herself and Parker. Now, she just wasn't in the Christmas spirit. There was this hollow spot in her chest and nothing seemed to fill it.

She just wanted to go home and curl up on the couch with Odie. Instead of Christmas movies, maybe she'd watch some romcoms. Then again maybe she'd watch a crime drama. Yes, that sounded much better.

As she approached the door of the community center, it opened before she reached it, and two teenagers barreled past her. They didn't seem to notice her. She grabbed the door handle before the door could close.

When she stepped inside, she was surprised to see so many people. Christmas music playing in the background got lost in the murmur of voices. People were festively dressed in ugly Christmas sweaters, reindeer antlers, and a couple had on Rudolph noses. She felt underdressed in her snowflake sweater. She reminded herself she wasn't staying, so it didn't matter.

With the bags of pretzels in each of her hands, she headed for the kitchen area. As she worked her way through the room, numerous people stopped her and asked about Odie. She was so grateful to be able to tell them he was doing well. Each day he was a little more like himself.

When she made it to the busy kitchen, she held up the bags. "I have the pretzels."

Merry smiled at her. "Thank you so much for picking those up. I appreciate it."

"Not a problem. But I should be going."

"Going? But you signed up for the contest." Merry held up a clipboard and pointed. "I have your name right here."

Belle inwardly groaned as she pasted on a smile. "I forgot about that. But I'm sure nobody will notice if I skip out."

"Oh. But you're wrong. Your partner will notice."

"Partner?"

Merry nodded. "We decided to switch things up this year. We're having two-person teams to work on each house."

There had to be a way out of this. Belle grasped for the first excuse she could come up with. "But I don't have a partner."

"Oh, you don't have to worry. We matched people. In fact, your partner is at..." She glanced at the clipboard. "You can find him at table thirty-four." And then Merry checked her gold wristwatch. "You better get to your seat. The competition starts in five minutes." When Belle didn't immediately move, Merry said, "Go ahead. I can't wait to see what you create this year."

Before she could respond, Merry moved away to speak to her husband. Belle's gaze moved to the counter closest to her. There were bowls of colorful gumdrops, peppermints in both red and green, and so many other candies. She had to admit that she could decorate a mighty fine gingerbread house with all of that. In fact, last year she won this very contest.

"Hey, Belle." When she turned, Candi smiled at her. "Are you going to participate?"

"I'm thinking about it." She glanced around. "Is Holly here too?"

"I haven't seen her. She might be home with Tater Tot," Candi said. "You should stay. I need some real competition."

Belle continued to hesitate. She thought of Odie, who'd been outside for a short walk in the snow, and had his dinner was waiting for him when he woke up. He would be good for a little while.

And maybe this was what she needed to get her holiday spirit back. *Yes.* This was exactly what she needed.

"Okay. I'll participate, but I have to warn you that I'm going to win." She sent Candi a teasing grin.

Candi's eyes widened, and then she smiled. "We'll see about that."

Belle glanced around the room. "I just have to find my table and find out who they partnered me with. I'll see you later."

As Belle walked away, her gaze scanned the numbers on the center of the tables. She was midway to the back of the large room when her gaze strayed across number thirty. She was in the right area. She picked up her pace.

She spotted thirty-one, thirty-two, thirty-three and at last she spotted thirty-four. She lifted her gaze to see who she'd been partnered with. Her gaze met mesmerizing brown eyes. Her heart fluttered in her chest. It was Parker.

Part of her said to turn around and leave, but the other part of her wanted to know why he was sitting at her table. Her feet made the decision for her when they started in Parker's direction.

When she reached the table, she asked, "What are you doing here?"

"To tell you the truth, I'm not sure. I got a call from Mrs. Kringle that they needed me here. But when I arrived, no one knew why she'd called me. When I tracked down Mrs. Kringle, she said that everything was taken care of and that since I was here, they needed one more person for the gingerbread contest. And you know how she can be. The next thing I knew I was sitting here."

Belle pulled out a chair and sat down. "That's pretty much how I ended up here too. Except my story involves pretzel sticks." And then she recalled the roses. "Thank you for the roses. They're beautiful."

"How'd you know they were from me?"

She shrugged. "You're the only one I know who would do something that sweet."

He smiled. "I'm glad you liked them."

Just then a bowl of the pretzel sticks she'd bought for Merry was placed on the already crowded table.

"Pretzels, huh?" In a perfectly straight face, Parker asked, "So, are we allowed to eat the decorations?"

She couldn't tell if he was being serious or not. Then he grinned at her, and they both let out a little laugh. It felt good. She hadn't laughed all week. Maybe she'd been missing him more than she'd been willing to admit to anyone, including herself.

Parker reached out and took a pretzel. The next thing she knew, it was in his mouth.

"Parker, stop. You can't eat the decorations. They won't give us anymore."

Parker looked at the bowl. "I didn't know." Then his attention turned to her. "So, does this mean we're doing this?"

She eyed up the table, noticing that they'd included Twizzlers this year and a few other candies. She did have a title to defend after all. And she liked the idea of spending a little time with Parker.

Before she could change her mind, she nodded her head. "Let's do it."

The smile slipped from his face. "In all fairness, I must confess that I have no experience with frosting."

She suddenly worried that this was his excuse to get out of the contest. "It's okay. You don't have to build the gingerbread house. You can go."

There was a momentary look of relief on his handsome face. But soon it was replaced with worry lines. "But what about you?"

She shrugged. "Maybe I'll go home to Odie."

"But you can't. You have a title to defend."

A little smile played at the corner of her lips. "So, you heard about that."

"I might have. I might also have been shown some pictures of the castle-like structure that you built. It was impressive. I can see why you won."

She let out a little laugh. "Thanks."

"So, I'll stay and build a gingerbread house if you will." He looked expectantly at her.

She didn't say anything. She was torn about what to do.

As though he could tell she was on the fence about the decision, he said, "We should make this interesting."

"What do you have in mind?" She was almost afraid to know the answer.

"We'll make a wager." He paused as though he could just pluck the idea from the air. "How about this? We each have to pick what place we'll finish. If my number is closest, you have to go have some hot cocoa with me at the Kringle Cup Café. If you win, I'll leave you alone to enjoy your holidays."

Ouch. She wasn't so sure she wanted to win this contest, but she wouldn't mind spending some more time with him. "Okay. Let's do this."

He blew out a breath. "Good. You have to name what place we'll come in."

She paused to give it some thought. Parker appeared to have never done this before. That would put her at a disadvantage. "I think we'll place third."

His brows rose in surprise. "You seem pretty confident."

"I am. How do you think we'll do?"

He pursed his lips, as though giving the decision some serious consideration. "I think we'll place seventh."

"You don't have much faith in our abilities, do you?"

Before he could answer that question, Merry stepped up on the little stage at the end of the room. "Welcome, everyone, to our annual gingerbread house decorating contest. As you noticed, we've switched things up a bit this year. Everyone has a partner so those houses should be twice as nice. You can use anything on your table to create your amazing gingerbread house. You'll have two hours to create it. And now because I know you all are anxious to get started... Begin. And good luck."

A frown pulled at Belle's lips as she looked around. Everyone was already busy assembling their houses. She was going to have to plan quickly and implement even faster.

"What's wrong?"

She glanced over at Parker, and their gazes caught and held a moment longer than was necessary. It made her heart skip a beat. Heat rushed up her neck and settled in her cheeks. She glanced away.

She'd meant to ask him something, but she couldn't recall what it was. Maybe that was because her heart was now racing, and all she could think about was how good he looked with the scruff trailing down his strong jawline and that cream-colored sweater paired with a pair of faded jeans.

"Belle?"

Oh. Right. Focus. And then it came to her what she'd been about to ask him. Her gaze lifted and briefly met his. "Do you have a pen?"

He smiled. "This sheriff always has a pen." He reached into his coat and produced a pen. As he handed it to her, he asked, "What do you need it for?"

"This." And then she started to draw on the disposable white tablecloth.

He leaned in closer. "What are you drawing?"

"An octagon."

"I know I'm going to regret asking this but why?"

"Because our house has to be distinct to win. So maybe an igloo house." She continued to draw out her idea.

After she'd drawn most of it, he said, "Don't you think that's a lot of pieces to hold together. And the roof... It looks complicated."

She hated to admit it, but he was right. With a frustrated huff, she leaned back in her chair. She needed something easy but would give the appearance of being complicated.

"I'm sorry." His voice held a conciliatory tone. "Your plan looks amazing. I just don't know if I can help you build something so intricate. Sometimes, I'm all thumbs."

"You're right. It's too complicated for the time we have to build it." And time was ticking.

She had another idea. She pointed to the table. "Take all of the candies off that baking pan."

As he followed her instructions, he asked, "Why?"

"You'll see." She grabbed the scissors and started to cut a portion of the paper tablecloth.

Parker gave her a puzzled look, but she ignored him as she continued to work. Once everything was off the metal baking pan, she turned it over. Then she smeared some of the white frosting on it before adhering the paper table cloth to it.

"What is this?" Parker peered at the beginning of her creation.

"This is going to be the yard for our gingerbread house. With only two hours to complete it, I can't go all fancy with the house design, so I thought we could embellish the yard."

"Are we allowed to do that?"

"She said we could use anything on the table, didn't she?"

He nodded, but he still didn't look convinced.

"Do you want me to ask Merry?"

He hesitated. Then he shook his head. "Let's do this."

Instead of debating the right and wrong of spending her evening with Parker, she just let herself enjoy the time. She already knew he was good in the kitchen, so it wasn't a big surprise that he was helpful building the gingerbread house.

Although, there was a part of her that didn't want to make the house too fancy. She found herself not wanting to win their bet. The thought of Parker avoiding her left a sour feeling in the pit of her stomach.

So, was it a total accident or did she subconsciously make a mistake when she cut the walls of the house? And then when she went to put the walls together, she didn't use enough frosting, and the walls fell down. One of the walls cracked in half. Thankfully, they had more gingerbread.

These mistakes were so unlike her because she was good at cake decorating. But every time she glanced over at Parker, she would lose her train of thought, and her stomach would dip. She inwardly groaned. This was going to be a long evening if she had to redo every step.

Chapter Twenty-One

NOT TOO BAD.

In fact, it was kind of cute.

As they finished the gingerbread house, Parker was truly impressed with what they'd done. Belle's idea about creating a yard for the house was a great one. And when he'd glanced around at the other tables, he found that no one was doing anything like their concept.

Belle had done such a good job with the house that he wouldn't be surprised if it took first place. And then he recalled their bet. If their house took the blue ribbon, Belle would win their bet, and he would honor their wager. But the thought of not spending time with her ruined his good mood.

As they continued to work together, he found Belle relaxing, and he did his best to hide the fact that he was worried about losing the bet. It wasn't hard, because Belle was engrossed with decorating. He was totally captivated by her artistic skill. He could just sit back and enjoy watching her work her magic.

But he didn't have time for that, because he'd been tasked with putting shingles on the house.

He glanced around the table, trying to decide what to use for shingles. And then he had an idea.

He reached for a bowl of frosting and another bowl of red and white peppermint candies. After giving the frosting a stir, he smeared some on the roof panel. Then he reached for the candies. He unwrapped the first one.

"You could also use the red candy wafers." Belle pointed to the full bowl.

His gaze moved between the wafers and the peppermint candies. He thought the peppermint ones were fancier. "Thanks, but I think I'll stick with these."

Instead of arguing her point, Belle merely nodded and went back to creating candy trees in the yard. "Maybe I'll make a shrub with the red wafers."

"That's a great idea. You're very creative."

"Thanks. I have a stroke of genius every now and then." And then she let out a little melodious laugh.

For a time, they worked in silence. Merry called out to let them know there were only fifteen minutes left. Time was quickly winding down. The rush to the finish was on. A hush had come over the entire community center.

He only had a few more candies to place on the roof when Mrs. Kringle headed toward the stage a final time. *Oh, no.* He had to finish this. He couldn't let Belle down.

He rushed to open the remaining candies. When he went to place them on the roof, his hand bumped the other side of the roof that was completed. The roof slid off to the side. The breath hitched in the back of his throat.

Before it could collapse, Belle caught it. "That was a close one."

"Sorry. I was in a hurry."

In the background, Mrs. Kringle was speaking to one of the judges. And then as he was placing the last candy, he heard her say, "Time is up."

He pulled his hand back and inspected his work. *Not too bad.*

"Congrats to everyone," Mrs. Kringle said. "You created the cutest gingerbread houses."

"I don't know about that," someone in the crowd shouted.

"Yeah," said another, "mine collapsed."

Mrs. Kringle sent them a reassuring look. "In some cases, it is truly the effort that matters. Everyone, give yourselves a pat on the back." She paused. "Now it's time for the judging to begin. Please, move away from your houses and have some refreshments. We have a huge cookie table. And if there aren't any thin mint cookies left, you have my apologies."

After Mrs. Kringle stepped off the stage, Parker looked back at the gingerbread house, and he noticed the one roof panel wasn't on straight. If he remembered correctly, it was the one that he'd bumped with his hand. If he could see it, he was certain the judges would see it too. And what was even worse was the panel was sinking on one side. He hated that he was letting down Belle.

She had fun.

She truly did.

Belle found herself smiling most of the evening. Parker had been good company, but then again, she already knew he could be a great guy—when he wasn't writing her a ticket. Then again, maybe that contentious relationship was in their past. She could only hope.

After waiting in a long, slow line, she munched her way across the cookie table. It was only after she grabbed another couple sugar cookies that she realized she had missed lunch because business was so busy at Frills & Heels. And then Merry had called her over to the community center before she'd been able to get dinner. But the melt-in-her-mouth cookies had taken the edge off her hunger. Then again, she could go for a couple more cookies.

She got back in line. After she completed her second perusal of the cookie table, she stretched her neck and looked around for Parker. She noticed him talking to the Wallaces. When his gaze caught hers, he excused himself and made his way over to her.

He eyed up the cookies on her napkin. "Did you save some for anybody else?"

She gaped at him. "I can't believe you said that."

He sent her a teasing grin. "I'm just giving you a hard time."

"I know. That's what shocked me. So, you aren't serious all of the time?"

He let out a laugh. "You still have things to learn about me."

"Apparently I do." She was looking forward to peeling back all of his layers and learning all about him.

Wait. Did that mean she wanted to continue seeing him? Her heart pounded a definite yes, but her mind cautioned her to be careful. Losing someone else she loved would be utterly devastating.

Parker's gaze met hers. There was something in his eyes. Was it interest in her? And then his gaze dipped to her lips. Suddenly, she felt heat start in her chest and work its way up to her face.

She glanced away. "You know," she said, ignoring the way her heart was beating double-time. "We did so well with our house that we might actually place in second."

"Second? What's wrong with first?"

She shook her head. "I saw a pink one with snow-covered trees. It's going to take first."

"I guess we'll find out soon. I think they're almost done judging."

A little bit later, everyone was instructed to make their way back to their table. Belle smiled. This was it. They would find out where they placed.

However, when they reached their table, she found there was a partial roof collapse. Belle gasped. This wasn't good. Not good at all.

When she looked over at Parker, he glanced back at her. And then the corners of his lips lifted. And the next thing she knew, he was laughing. How could he? This wasn't funny. All of their hard work was for naught.

Her gaze moved to the sad little house. And then she glanced back at him as he continued to laugh. The corners of her mouth lifted upward, and then she broke out in a laugh.

People gave them dirty looks for disrupting the award ceremony. Belle pressed her hand to her mouth to hold in her merriment. She felt good to be laughing. It felt as though she were expelling all of the negativity, and she was letting in the good. She felt lighter than she'd felt in a long time.

After they'd gathered themselves, she leaned over and whispered, "So, what happens to our bet when we come in last? Does it nullify it?"

He whispered back, "Doesn't matter. I'll treat you to a cocoa anyway."

It wasn't a good idea, but when she opened her mouth, she said, "Sounds like a plan."

"Good. Are you ready to quietly slip out of here?"

"Yes."

He reached out and took her hand in his. It felt good to have his fingers wrapped around hers. She told herself it was no big deal. It was something friends might do.

As she walked him out of the community center, Belle felt the protective walls around her heart coming down. She had missed him so much.

The Kringle Cup Café was just down the street. It wasn't worth driving there, since it would be hard to find a parking spot with so many people in town for the contest. She didn't mind walking, especially with their fingers laced together.

There was a light snow falling from the darkened sky. She watched the flakes flutter and dance through the air. She had a feeling she was going to remember this evening for a very long time. But would she remember it as the evening she passed up a chance to be happy for the rest of her life because she was too afraid to take a chance with her heart? Or would she remember this night as a time she was brave enough to go after her heart's desire?

"Parker, wait." She came to a stop.

He turned to her. "What's wrong?"

"Nothing. I mean, I need to apologize. I...uh, I freaked out after Odie came home. Until that moment, I had refused to acknowledge how scared I'd been. It... It brought back bad memories about my parents' accident. And I'm sorry I didn't handle it any better."

He reached out to her. The breath stilled in her lungs. As the snow continued to fall around them, it was like the world fell away. It was just the two of them in a snow globe.

And then his fingers lightly traced down her jaw as he stared into her eyes. "I'm sorry you had to go through that."

She couldn't look away from him. She felt as though she were drowning in his chocolate-brown gaze.

And then he lowered his head and claimed her lips with his own. His touch was gentle, as though he wasn't sure if she wanted this. Her heart pounded. It was so loud it echoed in her ears.

As his mouth moved over hers, she kissed him back. At the same time that his kiss exhilarated her, it also scared her. Putting her heart on the line wasn't something she'd allowed herself to do in the past.

And then Parker came into her life, and those protective barriers she'd kept firmly in her life were blown away. Now she felt as though her heart was naked and exposed. He had the power to love her or reject her. It was a precarious place to be, but she wasn't going to back away—even if it meant the pain of rejection.

The loud rumble of an approaching snow plow had them drawing apart. When he looked into her eyes this time, he was smiling. She smiled back at him.

"Still up for some hot cocoa?" he asked.

"I am."

He took her hand in his like they'd done it a million times before, and they continued along the sidewalk that now had a trace of snow over it. She lifted her gaze to notice the rooftops were also covered with snow. The street lamps all had big red bows. And every storefront had their picture window decorated for the holidays. That was one of the things she loved about her hometown—they were passionate about the holidays.

A block later they came to a familiar building with red-and-white-striped columns on either side of the front door. They looked a bit like candy canes. A wooden sign above the door was painted white with red lettering that read: *Kringle Cup Café*.

She peered through the large picture window next to the door, and the place didn't appear to be busy at the moment, but she was certain once the contest was over that people would flood the place.

They both ordered hot cocoa with little marshmallows. Once they were seated at one of the tables by the window, she didn't know what to say. She figured this must be what it was like to be tongue-tied. Still, she had to say something...

"I just..." she said.

"You know..." he said.

They'd both spoken at the same time. They both stopped at the same time and smiled at each other. She loved how his smile smoothed the frown lines on his face and how his brown eyes would twinkle.

Now that her panic over Odie's dognapping had subsided, she felt stronger and willing to take a chance on love. She wanted to take that chance with him. And if she read that kiss correctly, he wanted the same thing.

She opened her mouth to try again.

Buzz.

Parker held up his finger for her to wait a moment. He pressed the phone to his ear. "Bishop."

Interruptions were to be expected. After all, he was the sheriff. She was certain his life was interrupted on a regular basis. She would get used to it. But this time it was really, really bad timing.

By the little lines that once again bracketed his eyes and mouth, she knew the call was serious. As she picked up the bits and pieces of the conversation, she knew it was bad. People were hurt. Her words would wait for another time—a better time.

When he disconnected the call, he looked at her. "I have to go. There's a big accident on the highway."

She nodded. "Can you come over for dinner tomorrow?"

He sent her a brief smile. "I'm really sorry about leaving. And yes, I would love dinner." He got to his feet. "Message me what you need me to bring." He was already headed for the exit.

"Just bring yourself," she called out.

Without a backward glance, he was out the door. She didn't know if he'd heard her. As she settled back in the seat, her thoughts rewound to the snowflake kiss they'd shared. It was the most amazing kiss she'd ever experienced. She definitely wouldn't forget it.

And now they were going to have a Christmas Eve date. It didn't get much better than that. Maybe she should find herself some mistletoe. *Oh, yes.* That sounded like a really good idea.

Chapter Twenty-Two

H E HADN'T BLOWN IT with Belle.

Had he?

Parker hated running out on her. He felt as though they were getting somewhere when his phone had gone off. Talk about the worst timing ever. And as much as he loved Belle, he had to answer when he was needed.

It was the middle of the night by the time Parker relinquished the accident scene to his deputy. It was a bad scene—six cars and one tractor trailer that couldn't stop on the icy roadway. He always felt like he just couldn't do enough when he showed up at those tragic scenes. Thankfully, there were no fatalities, so he would take that as a win.

He'd been so busy all evening that he hadn't had much of a chance to think of Belle. And that was saying a lot. She was all he'd been able to think about since he pulled her over for her burned-out tail light. A lot had happened since then.

As he pulled into his driveway, he recalled their snowy kiss. It seemed like so long ago that he had held her on the sidewalk and kissed her. He had a feeling when they'd sat down to drink their cocoa that she had something important to tell him. He couldn't help but wonder what she'd wanted to say.

He thought of calling her—of wanting to hear her sweet voice to wash away the brutal images from the accident scene. When he reached for his phone, the time flashed on the screen: 12:23 a.m. *Um, yeah, I can't call her*. At least one of them would get a good night's sleep.

He was too wound up to sleep, so he got a hot shower, and then he went downstairs to finish attaching the last glass pieces to the ornament. And then he was going to spray them with clear acrylic to help hold everything in place.

Now that he was having Christmas Eve dinner with her, it would be the perfect time to give her the ornaments. He just hoped she liked them.

The most important dinner of her life.

At least, that was the way it felt.

Belle had gone into town first thing in the morning. She had Christmas shopping to do. What was she supposed to buy Parker? Her mind drew a total blank.

A wave of panic surged through her. She'd invited him over for Christmas Eve, and now she didn't have a gift for him. She wanted to get him something special, but she had no clue what that might be.

She'd walked through the men's store. She checked out the clothing. Nothing jumped out at her. She went to the hardware store, but she had no idea what tools he already owned and what he still needed. Maybe next year she would know these sorts of things.

The thought stopped her in her tracks. Would they be together next Christmas? Were they even together now? She had so many questions and absolutely no answers.

When she passed in front of the card shop, she slowed down. The Christmas tree in the window with its white lights and multitude of colorful ornaments on its branches called to her. The next thing she knew she'd moved to the front door. Her hand wrapped around the brass door handle, and she pulled it open.

She stepped inside the cozy shop. There was the pleasant scent of cinnamon, citrus, and cloves in the air. It drew her farther into the shop. There were so many shelves and stands with things for her to check out.

She thought of getting Parker a Christmas card, but she had no idea what tone it should take. A romantic card might be putting the cart before the horse. A friendship card just didn't seem like enough after what they'd shared. And then there were funny ones, but those didn't feel right either.

The next thing she knew she was in the aisle with all of the beautiful ornaments. She stood there, taking them all in—reminded of the heirloom ornaments that had been destroyed during the break-in. Those ornaments had meant the world to her, and she missed having them on her tree.

She stepped farther down the aisle. She saw an ornament that reminded her of Odie. She picked it up and took a closer look. It was as though this ornament was telling her to buy it for Parker. Even if after this dinner they went their separate ways, he would have this ornament to remind him of the Christmas he rescued her furbaby. Yes, this was the right gift. It was simple and yet meaningful.

With the perfect gift in hand, she rushed home. Odie met her at the door. When she picked him up, he gave her a great big sloppy kiss. And her heart was full of love.

Belle rushed to the kitchen. She started by making a pecan pie for dessert. And then because she didn't know if he liked nuts, she decided to make something else. But what? She flip-flopped a half-dozen times before settling on a chocolate cake. It would have to cool before she could frost it.

She roasted a turkey breast seasoned with herbed butter and plenty of rosemary. And then she'd pulled out her mother's recipe for stuffing. Because this was last minute, she'd had to tear the bread up, put it on a baking sheet, and dry it in the oven. Not ideal but it would have to do. She prepared potatoes until they were creamy and light. There was homemade gravy from the drippings from the turkey. And roasted carrots.

She checked the time. It was late in the afternoon. Parker was supposed to be there after his shift ended at five. She rushed upstairs to do her hair and makeup. Then the hard part was figuring out what to wear.

Should she dress up? After all, it was Christmas Eve. Or should she play it casual with jeans and a sweater? And if she dressed up, should it be a dress? Or slacks? There were so many choices.

She tried on a few outfits and promptly discarded them on her bed. She dug to the back of her closet and stumbled over a deep-red sweater dress. She studied it a moment. She'd had it for a few years, but she'd only worn it once. It still looked new.

She pulled it out of the closet. She didn't know why she hadn't worn it more. It was very comfortable, and yet it looked nice. She wondered if it would still fit her.

She took it off the hanger and tried it on. Then she stepped in front of the mirror. She gave her image a once-over. It fit. And it looked good on her. It was the winner.

A timer went off in the kitchen. She glanced at the mess of clothes on her bed. She would deal with it later. Right now, she had a cake to frost. Parker should be there any minute.

She rushed downstairs and glanced around. It was only then she realized she needed to plug in the Christmas tree and turn on the flameless candles in the windows. In the kitchen, she lit a bayberry candle that was on the island.

She whipped up some chocolate frosting and just finished frosting the cake when she heard a knock at the door. *Oh, no. He's here.*

"Arf! Arf! Arf!" Odie raced to the front door, barking the whole way.

She placed the empty bowl in the sink and quickly inspected the cake. On her way out of the kitchen, she caught her reflection on the door of the microwave. She tucked a strand of hair behind her ear.

She rushed to the door and paused. She straightened her dress before picking up Odie, who was still barking. "Odie, hush."

Odie didn't pay her the least bit of attention as he continued to sound off. And then, hoping she didn't have any frosting on her face or in her hair, she opened the door.

Her stomach fluttered with nerves. A big smile pulled at the corners of her mouth. "Merry Christmas."

Odie stopped barking when he saw Parker. Instead, he started whacking her with his tail, which rapidly swished back and forth. It moved with such force his whole body was moving with it.

Parker smiled back at her, raising her pulse. "Merry Christmas to you too." And then his attention moved to Odie. He reached out to pet him. "Hello, little buddy." When Parker's gaze rose to meet hers, he asked, "Can I come in?"

"Oh." Heat from her chest set her cheeks aflame. She backed up, pulling the door wide open. "Come on in."

She noticed he had a big box wrapped in silver wrapping paper decorated with the images of multi-colored ornaments. She grew worried that perhaps her ornament wasn't enough. Maybe she should have gone back and gotten that royal blue sweater she'd noticed in the men's store.

After he took off his coat and boots, he walked to the living room. He placed the package beneath the tree next to the gift she'd gotten for him. His present dwarfed hers. Did size really matter?

He turned to Odie, who was seated beside him. Parker bent down and picked up her puppy. Just like they were old friends, Odie lathered Parker with kisses. She was a little surprised to see the big welcome Odie gave Parker. Apparently, she had good taste in men, and her pup agreed.

When Parker turned his attention to her, he said, "This place smells amazing."

"Thanks. I made a little something for dinner." No way was she admitting that she'd spent most of the day working on it.

"Just point me in the right direction." He placed Odie on the floor. "I'm starved."

At least one of them was hungry. At that moment, it felt as though a swarm of butterflies had invaded her stomach. "Right this way."

She led him to the dining room. Odie was right beside him. When Parker stopped, so did Odie. Parker looked at the dining room table, which was already set with one of her mother's white tablecloths with red poinsettias around the border. She'd put out her grandmother's china. For the centerpiece, she used a miniature Christmas tree with itty-bitty ornaments and two red tapered candles. Suddenly, she felt as though she'd tried too hard. What did he think?

She turned to him. "Since it's the holidays, I thought we'd eat in here."

He turned a smile to her. "It's beautiful."

She felt her face grow warm. "I just hope dinner is as good."

He made a show of inhaling. "If it tastes half as good as it smells, it'll be perfect."

Even though she objected, he insisted on helping her serve dinner. Odie followed them back and forth from the kitchen to the dining room over and over again, hoping some of the food would leap from the serving dishes into his mouth. He was such a beggar.

Odie was disappointed nothing fell for him to catch. Instead, Belle fed him his kibble just like she did each evening when she had dinner. The only problem was that he gobbled it down much faster than she ate her dinner. And then he lay at her feet, just waiting for something to fall into his mouth.

Belle was relieved to find the food was actually good—really good. Not that she ate much. Feeling bad for Odie, she ended up feeding him some of her roasted carrots. He loved carrots. With his belly full, he ran off to the living room, where he curled up with his stuffed lamb and blanket.

Belle found herself repeatedly glancing across the table at Parker, wondering when she should tell him that she was wrong about ending things between them. She had missed him and she was falling in love with him. Every time she thought those words, her heart would launch into her throat, choking off her ability to verbalize her feelings for him.

But she couldn't keep quiet all evening. She had this feeling that if she didn't make her move tonight, she'd lose her chance. After all, Sheriff Bishop was one of the most eligible bachelors in Kringle Falls.

She glanced over at Parker. He lifted a serving dish and went back for seconds. And there were plenty of leftovers to save her from cooking for a few days.

After dinner, Parker insisted on helping her clean up. It was so sweet of him. She was touched. When they both reached for the bowl of mashed potatoes, their fingers touched and lingered. She raised her gaze to meet his. The visual connection caused her heart to flutter.

Chapter Twenty-Three

SHE WAS DRAWN TO him.

The breath caught in the back of her throat. Belle didn't want this moment to end. Parker's fingertips traced over the back of her hand. As he continued to stare deep into her eyes, his fingers trailed up her arm, leaving goosebumps over her skin. His movement was slow and purposeful. Her heart felt as though it were going to pound out of her chest.

This was definitely the moment to tell him how she felt about him. But her mind and mouth were at a total disconnect. She helplessly continued to lose herself in his eyes, which were now the color of molten chocolate.

When his hand reached her shoulder, he kept going. His fingertips tickled the sensitive part of her neck, sending shivers throughout her body. And then his hand moved to the back of her neck. The next thing she knew, she was leaning toward him as he leaned toward her.

With her heart pounding wildly in her chest, he pressed his lips to hers. It didn't seem to matter that she hadn't been able to find any mistletoe.

She reached out to him. Her hands pressed to his chest and then slid up to his shoulders. She leaned into him as her arms wrapped around his neck.

The kiss went on and on. She never wanted it to end. She didn't want them to end. If she had any doubts before, she didn't now.

"*Arf! Arf!*" Odie squeezed between them.

With the greatest of regrets, they parted. Parker was smiling while Belle frowned at Odie. "I'm sorry," she said. "He must need to go out."

Parker nodded in understanding. "I'll take him out."

She shook her head. "You don't have to."

"I don't mind at all."

She put on Odie's little red snow boots, his red coat, and his red leash. Working in clothing, she made sure to keep him color coordinated. Then she leaned over and whispered in Odie's ear. "Be good. Please."

While Parker took Odie out, Belle turned on some Christmas music. She didn't know why she hadn't thought of the music earlier. She dimmed the lights and turned on the flameless candles on the fireplace mantel.

She glanced around. Was it too much? She didn't have time to decide, because the front door opened. A rush of frigid air flooded the room. It felt like another storm was brewing.

She rushed over to take Odie from Parker. She divested Odie of his winter gear. When she put him down, he ran back to Parker's side. It looked like her two favorite guys had bonded. She smiled. This Christmas just might end up being one of her favorites.

Belle clasped her hands together. "Which do you want: dessert or your present?"

Parker looked at her and arched a brow. "You mean I can't have both?"

"Of course you can." She felt flustered. "But which one do you want first?"

He pursed his lips as though he were struggling to make the decision. After a moment, he said, "I think we should open the gifts first. What do you think?"

She smiled. "It definitely sounds good to me."

He took her hand in his and led her over to the couch. Once she was seated, he knelt down next to the Christmas tree. He picked up both gifts. He handed her the larger one.

Her palms grew damp. What if she hadn't gotten him a big enough gift? Would he think she didn't care enough about him? Because that was far from the truth.

Once he sat down, she said, "Open yours first."

She lowered her gaze and bit her tongue to hold back apologies for it not being fancy enough. She should have kept looking for something bigger, fancier. When she lifted her gaze, he was already ripping off the paper, just like a kid. A smile tugged at the corners of her lips.

He lifted the lid on the box and moved aside the tissue paper. He stared at its contents for a moment. And then he dangled the ornament from his fingertip. "It's Odie, right?"

He got it. Her nerves settled, and her smile broadened as she nodded her head. "It is. With you helping me—helping to get Odie home—I just thought we should commemorate this special Christmas."

He lowered the ornament and looked at her. "I love it. And I will always remember this Christmas and the sweet puppy that brought us together." His gaze moved to the package on her lap. "Go ahead. Open it."

Odie jumped up beside her and attempted to bite the package. Parker picked him up and put him in his lap. While Parker pet Odie, she carefully slipped her finger beneath one of the folds and gently pulled. She did it again until the flap of paper was loose. And then she turned the package to repeat the process.

"What are you doing?" he asked.

She didn't understand the question. She hesitated. "I'm opening the present."

"By the time you get done, I'm going to be retired."

She frowned at him. "The paper is so pretty. I don't want to ruin it."

"Would you give it a yank already? It's wrapping paper. It's meant to be ripped and crumpled up. It's not like you're going to save it."

She stopped unwrapping it and arched a brow at him. "How do you know?"

"Know what?"

"That I'm not going to keep the wrapping paper."

He paused and studied her. "I can't tell if you're serious or just giving me a hard time."

"Maybe I like to save wrapping paper and reuse it."

His brows rose. "I...uh, had no idea."

It was her turn to smile. "I'm just giving you a hard time."

He blew out a breath. "You had me for a minute."

She didn't say it, but she was going to keep just a small piece of the paper. She wanted to remember this Christmas. It was a very special one.

Her fingers moved faster, loosening the paper. And then she set aside the paper. The box was made of plain cardboard with no markings—nothing to tell her what might be inside.

The top had been sealed with packing tape. Using her fingernails, she worked loose the end of the tape. When she had enough loose, she grabbed it and yanked.

With the tape off, the flaps opened, and she peered inside at a bunch of... Wait. Was that a white towel?

She sent him a puzzled look. "You got me new towels?"

He let out a laugh. "No. There's something in the towels."

"Oh." She gingerly lifted the towel.

Below it she found smaller towels wrapped around something. For him to go to all of the bother, they must be fragile. She moved with caution. She picked up the first item. She carefully unwrapped it. Inside she found a unique ornament.

A glass ball was covered in smooth bits of glass. They were in shades of pink, blue, green and white. She lifted her head and looked at him. "Are these pieces of sea glass?"

He shook his head. He hesitated. "You probably don't recognize them, but these are some of the broken pieces of glass from your heirloom ornaments."

She held the ornament up in front of her and looked at it. The ornament twisted back and forth, catching the light from the Christmas tree. "You made this?"

He shrugged. "Partly."

Tears rushed to her eyes. She blinked repeatedly trying to stem them. "I can't believe you did this."

His handsome face creased with worry lines. "I'm sorry. I didn't mean to upset you. I... I was trying to find a way to hang onto those heirloom ornaments."

She reached out to him. Her hand landed on his knee. She gave him a quick squeeze. "I love it. I can't believe you went to so much trouble."

"You do?" He blinked. "You really like it?"

She smiled and then nodded. "Looks like we were thinking along the same line when it came to presents."

He smiled too. "I guess we were. You'll find eleven more ornaments in the box."

She gaped at him. "Wow. You were busy."

"I just wanted to give you back a piece of your past."

"And now my past is mingled with my future." She pressed her lips firmly together. She hadn't meant to vocalize her thoughts. But it was too late now. She might as well tell him the rest. She set the box aside and turned to look directly at him. Her heart was pounding. "I..."

"Wait." He scooted closer to her. "I have something to say."

"No. I have something to say."

"I love you," they said in unison.

"You do?" she asked.

"I do. And you..."

"Yes, I love you." She smiled.

"This is the best Christmas of my life." He leaned down and claimed her lips with his own.

Who needed mistletoe after all? Her heart felt as though it was going to beat out of her chest. *He loves me.* Her feet felt as though they'd left the ground. He loved her. As the snow continued to fall outside, inside it was just the two of them creating the most magical Christmas.

Epilogue

*J*UNE, K*RINGLE* F*ALLS*

It was her birthday.

Belle didn't want to make a big deal of it, even if it was a milestone birthday. She was turning thirty.

When they'd talked briefly that morning, Parker hadn't mentioned it. She didn't even think he remembered. He had to work the evening patrol that day. Because of conflicting schedules, they probably wouldn't even see each other. And that was okay. She didn't normally make a big deal of her birthday.

Instead, it was going to be an ordinary Friday night. She'd just closed up the boutique and was headed home. Mavis was in Florida visiting her sister for the summer. She'd already called to wish Belle a happy birthday. And she'd told her where to find her birthday gift. It was in the office in the filing cabinet. Belle hadn't opened it yet. She was taking it home and opening it with Odie.

Belle was going to be in charge of the boutique for the next three months. She was to do the employee scheduling, and once she got Mavis's approval, she was to order the winter collection. It felt like Mavis was trying out this arrangement to see if Belle could handle the responsibility. Belle wouldn't let her down.

Perhaps Mavis would retire and let her buy the boutique. Of course, it could also be a bit of wishful thinking on Belle's part. Mavis loved the boutique, and Belle wasn't sure she would ever walk away from it.

Belle had been working at the boutique since she was sixteen. She'd been saving up her money for college. And then one tragic day, she'd gone from planning for college to figuring out how to survive on her own—how to keep the only home she'd ever known—how to feed herself. As soon as she graduated from high school, her part-time job changed to a fulltime position at Frills & Heels.

Her dreams stretched further than taking over the boutique. She had plans to modernize the boutique with younger fashions, and she wanted to expand the selection of accessories. In fact, when she wasn't working and she wasn't with Parker, she was creating a business plan.

But she wasn't working on it tonight. She was going to order pizza and watch a romcom with Odie by her side. Parker didn't normally work Friday nights. He'd volunteered to cover for someone. He'd apologized profusely, and she'd told him it was fine. But in all honesty, she was going to miss him. But she had Odie. He would snuggle with her and try to steal her pizza when she wasn't looking.

When she arrived home, Odie greeted her at the door. When she picked him up, he lathered her with kisses. A smile pulled at the corners of her lips as her heart swelled with love. Who knew a little fuzzball could bring her such happiness?

Buzz.

She put Odie down and fished her phone out of her purse. When she checked the caller ID, she found it was Candi. She pressed the phone to her ear. "Hey, Candi."

"Hi. I was wondering if you could meet me at the Kringle Cup Café."

Belle was confused. And then she wondered if Candi knew it was her birthday. "What's up?"

"I need some help. Merry Kringle has put me in charge of a fundraiser for a new animal shelter here in Kringle Falls. I need someone to bounce some ideas off of, and Michael isn't much help. Even though I'm at the beginning stages, I want to have some ideas planned out to present to her on Monday. So, can you meet me there at six?"

It wasn't like she had anything else to do. "Sure. Do I need to bring anything?"

"Nope. I just need you."

"Then I will see you there."

Belle walked over and settled on the couch. Odie jumped up and climbed onto her lap. As she petted him, she said, "Sorry, little guy. It looks like our movie is going to have to wait until later."

After touching up her makeup and her hair, she drove back into town. Parking was hard to come by. As she passed in front of the café, she was surprised to find a line of people waiting to get in the door. It looked like there were a lot of tourists visiting their small town on this beautiful summer evening. She hoped Candi had arrived early, or they might have to go some other place. And she would be bummed because they served her favorite latte.

As she slowly continued down the road, she saw a young couple walking down the sidewalk hand in hand. It made her think of Parker. She missed him. Even though she saw him the prior evening, it seemed like a long time ago.

She got out and moved to the sidewalk. She started in the direction of the Kringle Cup Café. When she reached it, she took a spot at the back of the line. A minute later, she heard someone call out her name.

She looked toward the entrance and saw Candi waving at her to skip the line. She must have gotten them a table. Belle could already taste the latte.

Still, walking past the line of people she knew felt awkward. She greeted everyone and apologized as she passed each of them.

When she stepped inside the café everyone yelled, "Surprise."

Belle gasped. What in the world? She looked around, seeing all of the colorful balloons and a banner hung behind the counter that read: *Happy 30th, Belle.*

Her friends, Candi, Holly, and Felicity, were grinning at her. Something told her that her friends had helped with this.

The next thing she knew, Parker was standing in front of her. With a big smile on his face, he said, "Happy birthday."

"But I thought you had to work."

"I might have told a little white lie so you wouldn't figure out that I was helping to plan this party for you." And then he kissed her.

It wasn't a long kiss. And it wasn't a peck either. It was something in between that let her know he loved her, and she loved him.

When she pulled back, she looked up at him with a smile. "Thank you for this. I can't believe you did all of this." She looked around at the colorful balloons and streamers. "How did I not know you were up to this?"

He grinned at her. "I can be stealthy when I want to be. So, you like it?"

"I love it." She lifted up on her tiptoes and kissed his freshly shaven cheek. "And I love you."

"That's good because this isn't exactly a birthday party."

She arched a brow. "What are you talking about?"

He reached into his pocket and pulled out a little blue velvet box. Before it computed what was going on, Parker dropped to one knee.

Belle gasped as she pressed a hand to her chest. Sure, they had talked about a future together, but she hadn't expected it to happen today.

Now, the man of her dreams was down on bended knee in front of her. His brown eyes were filled with love for her. Her heart pitter-pattered.

She honestly never thought this would ever happen for her—she didn't think she'd let it. Then, along came Parker, and he had her taking chances with her heart. And she had never been happier.

Parker held out the ring. It was a three-diamond ring in a princess cut and set in what looked to be a white gold band. The light caught the diamonds, and made them sparkle. But it was the man who was holding the ring that held her attention.

Parker was her best friend. He was her confidante. He was her safe spot. And she loved him with her entire heart.

He cleared his throat. "Belle, I'm so sorry Odie was taken, but if ever there was a case of something good coming from something bad, this is it. Although to be totally honest, I started falling for you when I changed your tail light. And now I can't imagine my life without you in it because I love you with all of my heart. I want to share my life with you." He looked her directly in the eyes. "Will you marry me?"

She nodded. "Yes. Yes, I will. I love you too."

With cheers and whistles in the background, he slipped the ring onto her finger. When he straightened, he pulled her into his arms and kissed her.

He pulled back. "By the way, happy birthday."

"And here I was thinking that I'd be having a quiet birthday. You certainly proved me wrong."

"Are you happy?"

"Very."

"Good." He kissed her again.

Keep reading Belle and Parker's story! Sign up for my newsletter and receive a bonus epilogue. Get your bonus epilogue HERE or visit JenniferFaye.com

Next up, another Bishop brother finds his happily ever after.

Veterinarian Colin Bishop has dedicated his life to helping animals. He's had a crush on Holly Berry since they were kids. She was the adorable girl next door. The time was never right for them to date, so they'd remained friends all of these years. Holly runs the Kringle Soap Co, and she has given up on men. However, this Christmas one special puppy will help two lifelong friends take a chance on love in PUPPY SMOOCHES & PEPPERMINT KISSES.

Afterword

Thanks so much for reading Belle and Parker's story. I hope their journey made your heart smile. If you did enjoy the book, please consider...
- Help spreading the word about PUPPY LOVE & SNOWFLAKE KISSES by writing a review.
- Subscribe to my newsletter in order to receive information about my next release as well as find out about giveaways and special sales.
- You can like my author page on Facebook or follow me on Bookbub.

I hope you'll visit Kringle Falls, Vermont again for the next book in the series, PUPPY SMOOCHES & PEPPERMINT KISSES. You don't want to miss updates on previous characters and their love interest.

Coming next is Holly Berry and Dr. Colin Bishop, DVM's story...

Thanks again for your support! It is HUGELY appreciated.

Happy reading,
Jennifer

About Author

Award-winning author, Jennifer Faye pens fun, heartwarming contemporary romances. With more than a million books sold, she is internationally published with books translated into more than a dozen languages and her work has been optioned for film. She is a two-time winner of the RT Book Reviews Reviewers' Choice Award, the CataRomance Reviewers' Choice Award, named a TOP PICK author, and been nominated for numerous other awards.

Now living her dream, she resides with her very patient husband with a spoiled kitty and a pampered pooch. When she's not plotting out her next romance, you can find her curled up with a mug of tea and a book. You can learn more about Jennifer at www.JenniferFaye.com

Subscribe to Jennifer's newsletter for news about upcoming releases, bonus content and other special offers.

You can also join her on Bookbub, Facebook, or Goodreads.

Also By

Other titles available by Jennifer Faye include:

BLUESTAR ISLAND:
Love Blooms
Harvest Dance
A Lighthouse Café Christmas
Rising Star
Summer by the Beach
Brass Anchor Inn
Summer Refresh
A Seaside Bookshop Christmas
A Lighthouse Snapshot
Inheriting Her Island House
A Brass Anchor Inn Christmas
Race to the Beach
The Art of Seashells – coming soon

KRINGLE FALLS:
Puppy Wishes & Candy Kisses
Puppy Love & Snowflake Kisses – coming soon

Puppy Smooches & Peppermint Kisses – coming soon

Puppy Hugs & Mistletoe Kisses – coming soon

THE BAYBERRY, VERMONT SERIES:
Christmas in Bayberry
Valentine's in Bayberry
Rumors in Bayberry
Springtime in Bayberry – coming soon

SEABREEZE WEDDING CHAPEL:
The Bride's Dream Wedding
The Bride's Pink Shoes
The Bride's Christmas Dress
The Runaway Bride's Vow
The Bride's Antique Ring

WHISTLE STOP ROMANCE SERIES:
A Moment to Love
A Moment to Dance
A Moment on the Lips
A Moment to Cherish
A Moment at Christmas

TANGLED CHARMS:
Sprinkled with Love
A Mistletoe Kiss

GREEK PARADISE ESCAPE:
Greek Heir to Claim Her Heart
It Started with a Royal Kiss
Second Chance with the Bridesmaid

WEDDING BELLS IN LAKE COMO:
Bound by a Ring & a Secret
Falling for Her Convenient Groom

ONCE UPON A FAIRYTALE:
Beauty & Her Boss
Miss White & the Seventh Heir
Fairytale Christmas with the Millionaire

THE BARTOLINI LEGACY:
The Prince and the Wedding Planner
The CEO, the Puppy & Me
The Italian's Unexpected Heir

GREEK ISLAND BRIDES:
Carrying the Greek Tycoon's Baby
Claiming the Drakos Heir
Wearing the Greek Millionaire's Ring

Click HERE to find all of Jennifer's titles and buy link or visit JenniferFaye.com

Made in the USA
Coppell, TX
15 October 2025